CAPITALISTS MUST STARVE

TRANSLATED BY

CAPITALISTS MUST STARVE

PARK SEOLYEON

ANTON HUR

TILTED AXIS PRESS

CONTENTS

SICKNESS

She's starved for ages.

No longer can she remember chewing food and feeling it travel down her throat. Spit pools in the corners of her lips without going over the rise of her tongue. Her dry throat itches whenever she tries to swallow saliva.

Trees. If she could put her hand down her throat, it would squeeze through the esophagus like it were pushing through a hole in a dead tree, and her guts would crumble like dried leaves. If she could reach all the way down, shoving a shoulder into her mouth, then her head, then the other arm...

I'd feel full. I'd be flipped inside out.

These thoughts bring a faint smile to Juryong's face.

But then my flipped stomach would feel empty, too.

Juryong, lying on her side, hugs her legs as if she truly is inside someone's belly. She longs for sleep, the only thing she has left, but starvation keeps her alert. Blood hardly seems to circulate in her brain, blurring the borders between dreams and reality. Eyes closed, she feels every tremor, and slowly begins to forget herself. Knowing, at the same time, that this feeling was proof she was still alive. She keeps hearing someone say: *Kang girl, hey, Kang girl.* It's hunger that makes her hear it, and hunger that prevents her from answering. Then the cicadas... the cicadas... the sound of the cicadas tear through the air. She's no longer sure if she's hallucinating.

Is it summer?

Her eyes close on her blurry vision. The cicada cries grate on her psyche and scatter patterns of light behind her eyelids. This light spreads like the veins of leaves before crumpling, again and again, never the same shape.

Footsteps.

The sound of footsteps used to make her sit upright. Greeting this sound with her back straight is the smallest, latest bit of resistance a starved person can offer.

But not today, I won't today.

Juryong rolls to her other side. Who is this that keeps saying they won't, instead of they can't?

"Kang girl. Hey, Kang girl."

With a shaky arm, Juryong pushes away the floor. The retreating floor swims in her vision. When she forces her unmoving legs toward her torso, a grunt overflows from her throat. Like an animal. An animal, but not a wild animal. Didn't the rabbits they raised at home make the same sound when they were harvested?

The footsteps pause. She raises her head.

PART 1

GANDO

1

"What do you think is the prettiest thing in Tonghwahyeon?"

"I think the rabbits."

Rabbits when they're born are ugly and wrinkly, but once their fur dries and they get fleshier, nothing in the world is prettier to Juryong. The white ones have red eyes that look like beads of jade, the black or spotted ones have dark eyes that look human. The yellow ones are usually cute all over, and it's impossible to pick out one feature. But rabbits aren't just cute when they are babies. They grow big and fluffy, into creatures Juryong thankful to have. Few beasts are as deserving of gratitude as rabbits. Without their fur, the winters of West Gando would be impossible to survive. The luckiest thing is how they have a new litter in a blink of an eye. Who could possibly starve in a world with rabbits?

Juryong never considered the gathering of rabbit food as difficult work. Come to think of it, winter is near, they must harvest some rabbits soon.

"Not things like that, not useful things, tell me about pretty things."

"I said rabbits because they're pretty, they're not pretty because they're useful."

Juryong's mother is amused at her daughter's rejoinder. "What else is as pretty as a rabbit in Tonghwahyeon?"

"Mama's hands."

Juyrong stares into the mirror as she answers. The hands in question are busily working Juryong's hair.

"Oh please, nothing pretty about my hands. Forget rabbits, they are uglier than rabbit's feet."

"No, they're pretty. Nothing in this world is as pretty as Mama's hands."

The hands smoothly applying camellia oil into Juryong's hair are, as their owner claims, not pretty. Even with the oil, Juryong can feel the calluses scraping at her hair and scalp.

"Mama, don't you feel like you want to cry when you see a pretty thing?"

"A ridiculous daughter you are." Her mother ties Juryong's braid into a neat bun and fixes it in place with a long hairpin. "Have you yet to figure out what the prettiest thing in Tonghwahyeon is?"

"You won't tell me the answer, so how would I know? I still think everything I said is true, but Mama doesn't think so. It's you who doesn't know yet."

Her mother has nothing to say. Her warm hands massage sleep into Juryong's mind. But if she drops her head her mother might grab her by the hair, which means she has to make an effort not to fall asleep. It's hard.

Her mother adjusts the angle of the mirror so Juryong can get a better look.

"Kang girl, open your eyes. Here's the prettiest thing in Tonghwahyeon, sitting right in front of me. Our Kang girl."

Blushing, Juryong covers up her embarrassment with belligerence. "Why do you keep asking me things if you're not going to listen to the answer?"

Wordlessly, her mother places a borrowed bridal headpiece on her daughter's head.

Juryong can't stop herself haranguing her mother in the mirror. "Prettiest in the world is one thing, what's the use of being prettiest in Tonghwahyeon?"

Her mother says nothing. Juryong fills the silence with her grumbling. "Being prettiest in Tonghwahyeon means little in West Gando, and you've got to be the prettiest in West Gando to have a chance at being a great beauty of Korea."

Like she's someone else, Juryong observes the young woman in the mirror as she looks this way and that, studying her bridal headpiece from every angle. Hardly a face that's the prettiest in her village, let alone all of Tonghwahyeon, but not exceptionally ugly either, and that's just fine. The thought makes Juryong smile. She turns to her mother.

"And are you really going to continue calling me Kang girl?"

"A Kang girl is a Kang girl, what else would I call you?"

"I've got to act like an adult from today onward. What would happen if you called me Kang girl in front of my husband's family, like calling your pet dog? Think of the shame it'll bring on both of us."

Her mother's eyes well up with tears. "I call my Kang girl Kang girl, what else do I call her?"

With that, they leap into each other's embrace, clinging to each other in silent sobs. Women must not cry out loud on a festive day. Her mother's hot breath travels from her ear down her clothes before cooling. Footsteps from the wedding party ring in the courtyard. The two separate as they quickly wipe away their tears and smooth down their clothes, avoiding each other's eyes.

Juryong's father slides open the door a little and pokes his head in.

"You need to come on out, it's all too much, they brought a palanquin and a pair of wooden geese and everything."

Her mother sighs. Juryong cranes her neck, trying to catch a peek of the bustle in the courtyard. There's a crowd gathered in their tiny courtyard and outside the narrow gate.

"Say goodbye and cover your face when you come out." That's all her father has to say as he slams the sliding door shut.

Her mother gets up, hesitates as she looks back at Juryong several times, and finally drags herself out of the room.

Alone, Juryong tries to calm her feelings but she can't keep her fingers from shaking. She wants time to stop, but she's also curious about what life would be like in a new village.

Her marriage age is later than most of her friends, due mostly to her family's lack of money, but it's hard for her not to blame her looks just a little.

Old as I am, it wouldn't have been too bad, these days, to stay unmarried and take care of my parents through their old age. My little brother is only nine after all, who will help Mama and look after my brother when I'm gone?

Having thought so little of marriage herself, the speed in which the arrangements were made surprised her and everyone else. Perhaps this is normal, but the groom's family was in a rush themselves, putting on this ceremony in just a month. Twenty is a shamefully old age to get married, and the groom himself only fifteen. Surely the in-laws had some hidden intent of their own in tolerating such an aged bride for their son, a thought that makes Juryong hesitate even more about setting out on this course.

How awful of Father to be so cruel, acting like he's putting out the trash, and how infuriating that Mama must bow in penitence every time the in-laws visit, embarrassed about having kept a daughter unmarried for so long.

The thought of this bridal headpiece crowning every girl in the neighborhood before landing on her own head makes her want to toss it away.

But what is a stupid little girl like me to do, I till the fields when they need tilling and get married when I need to get married.

The sound of the crowd outside makes the inside of the room feel quieter, and Juryong mutters "Damn" under her breath as she flops to the floor.

"Ready? Opening the door."

Her mother's voice. Juryong flails, and getting back up with her wide sleeves is like trying to stay afloat in the ocean. She manages to sit up and look in the mirror to see a strand of hair hanging down unbecomingly on her forehead like a rat's tail. Outside the door, a throat clears emphatically.

"Coming, I'm coming."

Juryong quickly slips her hands in either sleeve and raises them to cover her face. The door slides open, and she could just about see the courtyard with her half-covered vision.

No one better laugh at me, I'll kick them in the leg, wedding or no wedding.

And yet, as embarrassing as she is to herself, not a single person is laughing at her. No one else to help her with her dress, her mother takes the role of bridesmaid as she grabs Juryong's right arm to help her balance and whispers in her ear.

"Hold your arms higher, raise your elbows to your eyebrows."

Before she does as her mother says, Juryong sneaks a peak at the groom's side. A boy, solemnly wearing the groom's hat, stands stiffly by the ceremonial table.

"I thought he was fifteen, he looks as old as me."

Her mother pinches her arm slightly, making Juryong flinch over the step down to the courtyard. "Who said you can look at your groom before the rites?"

Juryong purses her lips behind the cover of her wide, raised sleeves.

Look how Mama acts all strict in front of the villagers when she was crying over me in the room.

"And your hair. Couldn't you keep it neat for even a moment?"

"Is that all you got to say to your daughter going off to get married?"

Juryong stuffs her feet into her new shoes on the step. Everything else is borrowed for the day except these shoes. Their perfect fit convinces Juryong her mother had picked them out.

Her mother grips more firmly than ever above Juryong's much-descended elbow. "Whatever I say," she mumbles, "you'll resent me anyway..."

They make brides cover their faces at weddings because the tears may come at any time. Juryong is sure of it, and raises her sleeves to veil her face again. Her mother, guiding her down the path Juryong cannot see, whispers again.

"Live well. All right?"

You live well, you old woman... But Juryong swallows the words.

Finally, she is standing across from her groom by the ceremonial table. Having quickly mastered the art of peeking over her sleeves, she could just about assess her husband to be taller than her, requiring a considerably upward glance to even approach that face over his shoulders.

Five years younger but this tall? What have I done while he did all that growing?

The thought amuses her so much her shoulders shake in suppressed giggles. Well, at least no one will make fun of him for being a boy groom.

From the house of Choi, they told her, and named Jeonbin.

What should I call him? Jeonbin-ah, and my in-laws would murder me. Husband, and I'll never stop myself from laughing. Why hadn't Mama told me what to do in this case? What does

Mama call Father again? Your father? What does she call him when she calls him directly?

She realizes her mother has never addressed her father in her life. What a disaster.

Juryong's father and a member of the groom's family pour a drink for Juryong and the groom. Their ceremony was to be simple, the groom's patriarch reading his congratulations and then exchanging bows and then shared shots of rice wine. This moment where she takes her cup is to be the first time she looks upon the groom's face. Her hands unclasp from each other as she accepts the cup from her father. The ache in her arms, which she had been too nervous to notice, registers for the first time. Afraid she'll drop the cup, she hastens it to her lips, but not before she quickly glances upward. *Gulp.* Her eyes widen.

"Ya, drink only half, weren't you just told?"

Juryong can't hear her father's scold. The sight of her groom's face made her down the whole shot without noticing. A face still retaining its boyish charm but with the clear lines of a man.

He might make a prettier girl than me should we switch clothes.

Her father refills her cup in a hurry because he needs her to leave half for her groom. The guests laugh. The groom suppresses his laughter as well and isn't wholly successful. Juryong should feel embarrassed, but the sight of her groom's beautiful face has filled her with warmth.

"Ya, don't smile! If the bride smiles on her wedding day, her first child will be a girl."

But Juryong can't help it, no matter what the guests say. They drink from each other's cups, Juryong unhesitatingly gulping down from where her groom's lips had touched, despite the disconcertion of her father.

★

It's late fall and the days are short, but the guests show no signs of going home.

The sound of her father dragging two drunkards out of the courtyard makes Juryong realize the wedding is over. For two hours she'd been sitting in this room with her groom with nothing but awkward silence between them. The neighborhood women who had sat on the porch right outside their door pretending to chat as they snuck glances at their room had irritated her, but now she wishes they were back just to break the tension.

All they had with them were their newlywed bedding and a little bit to eat and drink. Only two rooms in this house and they were given the better room for this occasion, but to think that it's her parents' room.

Burning with frustration, she fills her cup and glances at her groom as she takes a sip. He doesn't seem to know what to say.

Does he know what needs to be done? He looks petrified, like a child.

Sighing, Juryong takes off her own bridal headpiece. Better put that oil lamp out, the oil is precious. They used too much fuel in honor of her new groom and now the room is too hot. Jeonbin, taking his cue from her, begins undressing himself.

Huh.

Juryong loosens the front knot of her jeogori. Just as she's about to cast off her inner jeogori as well, Jeonbin covers his eyes with one hand and turns his head.

So he knows to look away from a woman's body, does he? Not a child, then.

This makes her want to tease him. In her underwear, she crawls underneath the covers of their bedding. Propping up her head with one arm, she speaks to Jeonbin.

"What can you be doing? It's cold, come here."

"I'm not cold."

"Going to sit there all night?"

Jeonbin reluctantly—or not so reluctantly—drags himself closer to her.

"Come inside."

Juryong gives the empty space next to her two firm pats. Jeonbin hesitates despite how close he is now. It irks Juryong.

"Does your bride displease you so?"

He vigorously shakes his head. "Not at all, at all."

The sight of him jumping back as he emphatically waves his hand *No* in the air makes Juryong suppress a smile.

"Then why would a pleased man wear such a face?"

He looks about to cry at her words.

His struggle to form his own makes her want to tease him again. "Soon you'll be kicking me out of your home and looking for a new wife."

It doesn't escape her notice how scandalized he looks. She hadn't cared too much about being deserted by her husband before meeting Jeonbin, but now that she's seen his face, she concludes that it would hurt a great deal. She wants to slap her own mouth for even joking about it. What to say to dispel the awkwardness? Cursing her fate, she is about to turn around to face away from him when Jeonbin speaks.

"There is a thing I swore with my night school friends. That I shall join the Liberation Army..."

Juryong sits right up and stares at Jeonbin. The bedcovers flung from her chest create a gust of wind that sways the flame of the oil lamp. Jeonbin stares right back into Juryong's eyes that have become as wide as rabbits' eyes.

"I'm a man who can't keep a sworn oath with his peers, ashamed I did what the elders ordered me to do, and now I'm sorry for my wife. I don't know what to do with myself."

Finally, the reason behind their quick betrothal.

So, they saw their baby boy wanting to join the liberation movement and decided to tie him down through marriage, did they? His desire and their fears battled against each other, and I'm the result.

A calm comes over her at this thought.

"That's no trouble at all. Don't worry, lie down."

Jeonbin rubs his eyes and stares at her.

Look how damningly handsome he is, even when he's sad. Lamenting inwardly, Juryong chooses her next words carefully.

"I understand how your elders feel and I understand my, what is it, *husband* also. Your mother and father aren't trying to stop you from doing big deeds. They just want to give you a little more time to grow, that's all."

He pouts. He already knows this.

"But I'm the same. Look at me. No schooling, no cleverness, just an ordinary woman. But I'm not stupid enough to stop my husband from pursuing big deeds. I would want him to pursue even bigger deeds, if anything." She drags the oil lamp nearer to their pillows. "The night is late so sleep for now, and I want to say, if you hate me so and don't think you can live with me, leave while I sleep. I won't hold you back."

Jeonbin doesn't move.

Well, if he won't join me under the covers after that, there's nothing I can do.

Juryong blows out the oil lamp and is about to pull the blanket up to her chin when she feels Jeonbin slipping in beside her. And a cold hand, gently tapping at her face.

"Your hand is cold."

"Sorry."

Why is he apologizing—and did I really say all that to him just now?

A delayed embarrassment overwhelms her as she turns away from him. But his creeping closer to her stokes her pity, making it impossible to keep her back to him. She turns and hugs him. He's taller than she is, but there's something still vulnerable about his body.

If I open my eyes in the morning and he's not there, I better not cry, or act upset.

With that thought, she dozes off. A tiring day for her young groom to be sure, but the wedding had been exhausting for her as well. They sleep through the night until the sunrays break the horizon.

Juryong is the first to wake. The sight of her husband's face as he sleeps with an arm around her confounds her. It is odd to have slept in the arms of a man she had only met the day before, ridiculous that such a man is her husband, adorable that his face even in repose is beautiful, and marvelous that she had truly gone through with getting married. But most of all, it's reassuring that Jeonbin had not left her in the long night.

Perhaps having a tense dream, his eyelids twitch from time to time. She notices there are six holes poked into the paper screening of the sliding door, with one of the fingers of light falling directly on his eye. Juryong stretches out a hand and blocks the light with her palm. She stares down at his sleeping, breathing face for a long time. Her mother's question from the day before suddenly comes to mind.

I know what's the prettiest thing in Tonghwahyeon. It's my husband.

The thought fills her with pride. There really is nothing like her husband.

2

"*Wife*, what does your name mean?"

"*Ju* for everywhere, *Ryong* for dragon."

"Ah, so you're meant to embrace the world with your long body."

"Do you think so? I don't even know how to write it in Chinese characters."

"The *Ju* in your name and the *Jeon* in mine mean similar things. My name, Jeonbin, means shine everywhere."

"What a pretty name."

"Don't call a man pretty!"

Juryong bursts out laughing at Jeonbin's retort. He always gets in a mood when he's not treated like a man or an adult. He doesn't realize that's exactly what makes him so childish.

"So, how long have you lived in Gando?"

"I came to Tonghwahyeon when I was fourteen."

"Before that, where? Where do you come from?"

"Born in Ganggye and raised in Pyongyang. It's not far from Ganggye. Lots of beautiful women are from Ganggye."

"That's why you're so pretty."

"Are your eyes on the bottom of your feet?"

Juryong covers her mouth—she didn't mean to speak so roughly. Jeonbin laughs softly. Sleep weighs on his voice. His questions continue.

"Why did you have to come to Tonghwahyeon?"

"That's what I want to know."

Unable to answer the question, Juryong falls deep into thought. They could've gone back to Ganggye or headed to northern Manchuria. Or Daemado Island or Russia. Only fourteen when she clung to her mother's skirts as they got on the train to Gando, she still doesn't know why they have to be in this strange land. They might have been running from something, the train being a night train—that is as far as she could guess. Mother and Father do not seem like people who would be on the run from something, but it's romantic to think so and Juryong had decided this was the story she would tell herself.

"You asleep?" Jeonbin asks.

Juryong thought he'd fallen asleep in her arms. She shakes her head on the pillow. The hair from her temples rustle and curl.

"What are you thinking about so hard?"

"That I came to Tonghwaheyon to find me a husband, why?"

She thrusts a hand in his armpit to tickle him and his giggles tickle her ears back so lovably that she embraces him tight. Still strangers to each other, the night doesn't feel long to either of them. When Jeonbin asks Juryong answers, and when Juryong asks Jeonbin answers. The two find no end to their conversation. Like they had waited their whole lives storing stories to tell each other and only to each other. They didn't know that the winter they'd held their wedding was coming to an end.

"When I was little, I was the eldest daughter of the owner of a big shop, we had respect. Now I'm a field hand, the best at gathering weeds to feed cows, the best at hoeing rows. Even the manliest of men sing praises at the mention of the girl Kang of the House Kang. Who'd believe I'd never so much as held a handful of dirt when I was a child."

"My darling had a harsh life."

"Yes, I had to grow up harshly."

"What're you going to do now that your groom is so young and weak?"

"Smash whoever says my groom is young and weak with these bare hands."

Juryong's joking leads Jeonbin into a slow smile. Despite the dark, she can feel his face move against her hand cradling his jaw.

So this is what marriage means, what being a couple means— it's gaining a friend. A friend who will never push me away or abandon me.

The thought swells her heart.

"No, my darling, I will grow up as quickly as I can and protect you."

Juryong grins in the dark. She doesn't hate what she hears but still finds it silly. This young boy is barely a year older than she was when she came over from Pyongyang to Tonghwahyeon.

Wait, since it's the new year, does that make him a year older now? The honest truth is that her soul is in constant conflict between wondering when he will grow into the man she needs him to be and wishing he would be this young and lovely forever.

"Where did you learn to talk like that? Do they teach it in your night classes?"

Her teasing elicits no reply. He must've fallen asleep.

★

The cock crows before the dawn. Juryong, cautiously as to not wake Jeonbin, slips out of the bed and puts on her clothes. Quietly she slides the door to leave the bedroom, closes it without a sound behind her, and goes directly to the jeongjugan big room. The first task she needs to do at every dawn is to check the furnace. Her grand aunt and nieces had slept there on winter nights, but now that they were back to sleeping in their rooms, it's easier to move about. She feeds the furnace with the pine kindling that had been hung dry, and soon the dying flames jump up once more. The water jar is about half full. She smashes the sheen of ice that had formed overnight and dips a gourd into it for water to pour into the iron cauldron. As she mixes in some rice with potatoes and barley, her sister-in-law rubs her eyes and yawns as she enters the room. Juryong leaves the cooking to her and goes off with the water bucket into the morning.

"The littlest of the Choi family is here!"

As early as Juryong is, there's already a line of women waiting before her. Their faces are still swollen from sleep but not a trace of slumber remains in their alert eyes. Only the young girls keep yawning and rubbing their eyes as they keep a wobbly grip on their buckets.

Juryong scoffs. "Me, the littlest? I'm older than my husband!"

"And being a newlywed?" teases one of the mischievous women. "Lots of fun?"

Juryong suppresses the urge to break into a smile and gives her answer in solemn modesty. "My husband is far too busy with his studies to be having fun."

"Your husband? Your play husband, more like."

Juryong glares at the woman who said this. The others giggle, and she wants to push them all into the well.

But I have to forgive them, I'm the one with the good husband. These other hen's roosters, they're no good against the Japanese, they're already called heroes if they don't beat their wives or children. Binnie, though, will save our country.

Feeling smug, Juryong busies herself with the water. She will need to make at least four trips to fill the water jar, she'll have to make it quick if she wants any breakfast.

The Choi household is, rare enough for a Gando home, an extended family. Generations of merchants mean they hadn't known hunger for a long time, but their family had fallen on hard times after some bad business. Jeonbin told Juryong his grandmother was pregnant with his father, and Juryong teared up despite her husband's restrained, emotionless retelling. This grandmother was like a tiger and especially mean to Juryong, but the thought of her as a pregnant young widow in tears as she entered exile in Gando made Juryong's eyes well up. They hadn't had railroads back then, so the journey must've been even more arduous.

"How does this household look to you, my wife?"

As Juryong hesitated to answer his careful question, Jeonbin continued the story of their family.

"As you can see, we haven't fixed our habit of silly pride in our lofty past. We're still ignoring the new world where there's no high or low in how you're born."

Juryong knew very well why his grandmother treated her harsher than her sister-in-law, Juryong's older brother's wife. The wife of her brother-in-law had been chosen with great care, as he's the eldest, and her family lived nearby, which made her husband's family more careful about mistreating her. But of course Jeonbin's family would be out for blood when it comes to the hastily procured wife of the second child. Every time she wants to shout that her family has roots as well, she bites back her words because she doesn't want to shame her husband, or her parents, who would be castigated for raising a bad daughter.

Roots, why are they even important? Was Lee Wanyong born a bastard before he sold out his country? No—he was the highest of the highborn, roots going down deeper than anyone else. A yangban, an aristocrat, a traitor to his country.

That's what she thought to herself whenever the grandmother clucked her tongue at her. Roots, huh. The dead grandfather would mix Chinese and Japanese words together whenever he got giddy from drink. Damn roots... Do they think her own family never had a time when their voices carried above everyone else's?

Her mother-in-law's nastiness is also more than normal, even if it pales in comparison to the grandmother's. This mother-in-law is quicker with her fists than her words, something Juryong's sister-in-law tipped her off to when she first moved into the house. Any little mistake of Juryong's is answered with a slap on her back, and while such mistakes are rare for Juryong as she's quick to learn and clever with her hands, her mother-in-law once chased her sister-in-law with an iron poker while the young woman was pregnant with her first child. When Juryong asked why her sister-in-law endured such treatment when she'd been raised under gentler circumstances and her family lived nearby, she said it was because she didn't want to bring shame on her mother.

After the family is fed and the dishes cleaned, Juryong puts on her jige carrying rack and heads for the mountains. They would need kindling throughout the night until May or June, and soon things will get too busy for her to go to the mountains, so she has to gather as much as she can now. A woman who carries around a jige on her back—another thing that grandmother harangued her about. But what was she to do when the last boy servant they had was let go years ago and no one else does the work? Juryong kicks a clump of dried grass on the side of the path as hard as she can.

Damn roots!

On the mountain, she sits on the trunk of a fallen tree to catch her breath and looks down on the village. At the well, the women gathered on the banks by the stream, there were people out and about, children who dart from place to place, the houses, walls, vegetable patches tucked in here and there, the shorn fields where some impatient folk had irrigated too early, the water then turned into ice like dull glass in the sun.

Everything looks smaller than her smallest finger. Small and silly. At this distance, she couldn't even remember what had irritated her so.

But when I go down to that village again, I'll become as small as well. And get angry at small things and cry and laugh at small things.

Such thoughts even distract her from thinking about her handsome husband. Unaware that this was loneliness, Juryong wallows in it for a moment like it's a patch of sunlight she's found. It's not a feeling she can indulge in for long.

Once she fills up the jige and quickly makes her way back home, she has to make dinner for her husband. She goes down the mountain so fast she might as well have rolled down the slope, but not a single twig falls from her jige.

She knows what she has to do next.

Go out to the riverbank to do laundry and then come back to dry it, grind the barley, shred and dry the radish, redo the earthen paint on the big room with some spare time, make dinner for the family, see Jeonbin off to his night school, light the night fires, see if anyone from Jeonbin's grandmother to her sister-in-law needs anything, then sit in her room, light a stove with pine fires and mend the family's clothes.

A good day of solid work.

With that thought, she begins to nod off. The tip of her needle wanders and pierces her hand. She hears her mother-in-law in the other room. "Child, lie down now, aren't you wasting fuel?"

"Yes, Mother, I am almost done." She rubs her eyes and continues with her work. Jeonbin is late, she thinks as she looks up, and sees clumps of white in the wind outside. Spring snow.

She takes out Jeonbin's padded jacket to meet him outside on his way back. Carefully, she steps on the fresh snow. Someone has opened and closed the gate. There are footprints outside leading up to the gate that turn away. It's obvious they are Jeonbin's.

Juryong senses abandonment. She runs back inside the room to get a lit pine branch to light her way through the snowy night.

On the path, his footsteps mix with those of others. She takes a moment to discern which of them in the mess are Jeonbin's. It looks like he went with a group of men toward the entrance of the village. She stops to take a breath. The night that descends on the vanishing footsteps ahead of her is as cold and dark as bottomless water. She spits out the snowflakes that fell on her mouth as she ran. Tears well. Just when her racing pulse finds its rhythm once more, Juryong manages to take a deep breath. Like a diving woman about to plunge into the depths of the ocean, she takes a step outside the village entrance.

"Where are you going?"

Startled by the voice, she drops her pine branch. It falls onto the snowy rice field by the path and the fire snuffs out. Jeonbin is right behind her. He must've been outside for a while, as his head and shoulders are piled with snow.

Juryong tries to calm herself.

"Never mind that, where has my husband been?"

"Home, but my wife wasn't there, so I looked for you outside."

Jeonbin sniffs. Juryong quickly dusts off the snowflakes from Jeonbin's padded coat she had brought with her and hands it to him. He takes it and spreads it over her shoulders instead.

"Dear Sir, it's meant for my husband."

"Why such formality, My Lady?"

Jeonbin, tickled at this unusual politeness, has a hint of laughter in his voice. Juryong doesn't answer but shrugs herself out of the coat. The coat lingers in the shape of her shoulders for a moment before folding over Jeonbin's arm. The coat folded by his side, Jeonbin looks back at Juryong without a word.

Juryong speaks every syllable slowly and clearly, trying to hold back the sobs.

"Where were you going without telling me?"

The clouds cover the moon, and the snow is in her face, making Jeonbin hard to see.

He is my one and only friend in the world.

The thought pushes hot tears down her frozen cheeks. "Sorry that I am so pitiful. I know nothing is as important to my husband as liberation, but I didn't know he would leave a bride he had lived with and shared affection with. Sorry that I am too weak a woman to let go of my husband who is destined to do great things."

"I..."

Juryong wipes her tears and waits for Jeonbin to finish his sentence. Only a word, and she could already hear the tears in his voice. More than her own tears, the fact of her husband's tears breaks her heart.

"I, I like you..."

She bursts into tears again. True they had lived together and shared the same bed for several months and were as affectionate as brother and sister, but this is the first time they had said words like "like" to each other.

It's unfair he says this to me now.

Jeonbin holds back his tears. "I like you, and I want you to live in a liberated country. I want to give you that life, by my own hand. And it is what I promised my comrades."

Juryong desperately wants to embrace her husband.

"But you came back."

Her voice breaks at the end, and Jeonbin finally begins to cry.

"I, I couldn't... my feet refused to let me leave my wife behind."

Juryong can't hold herself back anymore. She flings her arms around Jeonbin's neck. In the dark snowstorm he had been a looming shadow of a man, but in her arms he's the youthful lover she has always known him as, and this reassures her. Indeed, youthfully, Jeonbin can't stop crying once he's started.

"I'm sorry, I'm sorry. I'm the pitiful one, not you."

"Don't say that. Who dares call my husband pitiful?"

"I'm sorry I'm a pitiful husband."

"Pitiful or not, you're my husband."

She holds onto him tightly and pats his back and repeats herself over and over again. That pitiful or not he is her husband; that no husband of hers can ever be pitiful.

3

A secret between couples makes the distance between them great, but a secret shared by a couple makes them closer. Juryong knows that now.

Every exhaled breath turns white. The cock hasn't crowed yet. In the border between night and dawn, Juryong finally loosens her hold on Jeonbin.

"Let's go home now."

"Let's."

Who knew such a night was waiting for her when she got married? In all honesty, Juryong doesn't think much about country or liberation.

What's the use of liberating a country that fails to protect or take care of me? No business of mine what name my country has, as long as my family doesn't starve and isn't cast out into the cold.

That's how she thought. There is no pride in it, but no shame, either. Her insistence, now, that her husband take her where the movement takes her isn't because she believes in the movement but because she's worried for his well-being.

Whether he realizes this about her or not, Jeonbin does seem to consider her proposal earnestly. One evening, back from night classes, he hands her a workbook.

"You should know how to write the three syllables of your name, at least."

"But I do know how to write my own name…"

In Pyongyang, Juryong had followed her friends to church and lingered around the girls' schools, so she wasn't completely illiterate and could read haltingly. The problem was writing. The only letters she could write with confidence were, indeed, the three syllables of her own name.

"I'm told there are many women who are active in the liberation forces. There's nothing to stop you from doing the same. But you have much to learn and prepare before you do so."

Their nightly conversations turn into tutoring sessions. Once Juryong gets a good grasp of reading, Jeonbin borrows books for her. Some are novels and poetry, but he mostly brings home magazines or chapbooks with news of the liberation movement. They are about the Liberation Army, formed in southern Manchuria, attacking a Japanese police station in his hometown of Ganggye, triumphing over the Japanese army in Cheongsanri and Bongohdong. Juryong asks questions, and Jeonbin answers each one as vividly as if he had witnessed these events with his own eyes.

"Losing one's country is to lose our language, our spirit. Think if my name wasn't Choi Jeonbin but Matsuda or Takeshi."

But do I really care what name my husband has? If he were Takeshi of Japan or Wang of China, none of that matters to me, it only matters that he's himself.

She can't say this to Jeonbin. She doesn't want him to feel sad.

But when they receive news that the Japanese have massacred civilians and set fire to a village in northern Gando in the name of smoking out the Liberation Army, a fire flares up in Jeonbin's heart. Juryong understands how feelings like patriotism or a sense of justice must put down some roots into hostility as well. To think that their people, folks like their parents and little siblings, would've died these unjust deaths, while Juryong was too busy going about her day to hear the news, makes her sick with rage. And the thought that she, as well, could die like this at any time chills her to the bone. News like this makes her beg Jeonbin to never leave her behind should he go away.

One night, as they leave the door open behind them lest the sound of it closing is noticed by Jeonbin's grandmother, whose sleep has decreased much of late, the two of them run away. Juryong has to turn Jeonbin back on the path they take because he keeps stopping and looking back. Of course he feels more and more anxious the farther he gets from his blood. Who knows when they would see them again? If it becomes known he joined the Liberation Army, the Japanese will come down on the household. Throwing oneself into a great cause inescapably meant committing a sin against one's family. Jeonbin, Juryong, and some bits of gold the grandmother had hidden away have all disappeared—the shock would be considerable for the family.

"Where to now?"

"In the summer, the Liberation Army and militias in southern Manchuria got together to form a council. We have to go southwest for a long time. Comrades who made it there first will greet us."

"What's a council?"

Her question must've made his heart swell, as Jeonbin's grip increases in strength.

"A council means we've created our own government, even if it's provisional. A government mostly military, but still, a desire for a people to rule themselves."

How wonderful that he is the kind of person who would say such things with such light in his eyes. She squeezes back.

But to walk a hundred li in this late-autumn cold—they wear all the clothes they own and it's bearable for now, but their wrists and ankles and necks let heat seep out the way cracks in a jar leak water.

The rising sun only warms the tops of their heads as the wind continues to buffet them. In fear her nose will shatter like ice, Juryong holds up her scarf to her face. Her exposed neck, however, means she can't do that for long either.

"You're cold."

"No, but maybe my husband is!"

Juryong is quick to protest whenever Jeonbin apologetically asks her if she's cold. She knows he is only worried for her, but she's afraid he'd regret her presence by his side, so she puts on a brave face.

Her shoulders, knees, and every joint in her body feels like frozen hay. With every step, the creaking of her bones threatens to spill out of her mouth as moans, but she doesn't want to worry Jeonbin and barely even lets on she's out of breath.

The roads become narrower in the mountains. The couple moves out of the way at the sight of carriages or army jeeps. Any car that seems to carry a Japanese person makes Juryong feel as nervous as if they're already part of the liberation movement, afraid of getting caught.

"Don't worry. We just look like a couple looking for a new place to live and are too poor to take the train."

This reassures Juryong but also makes her realize he has the same nervousness.

It doesn't feel like they're joining an army as yet, it's more like some game. They are playing at being liberation fighters. The thought of her husband, the best man in the world, joining the liberation movement makes her feel liberation is going to happen tomorrow, or even after lunch, and even the hard road ahead seems so wonderful because they're together. She keeps smiling despite herself. It makes her blush to think Jeonbin read her thoughts.

Sometimes, I feel like I'm the young one here, not Jeonbin.

Not knowing why Juryong had quickened her pace to walk up to his side, Jeonbin automatically wraps one of his arms around her shoulders. Before them stretches a long and generous road.

"How many li have we walked?"

"I don't know, at least seventy."

As the sun turns from the south toward the west, elongating their shadows, Juryong and Jeonbin come upon a fork in the road with signs in Hanja, roman letters, and Japanese. Nothing Juryong can read. The sign pointing the way they came says thirty, which means something was thirty kilometers that way, likely the biggest town she and Jeonbin passed by, and ten li being four kilometers, they truly did walk over seventy li. Juryong's fingers cease their movement as she finishes her calculations.

"Hungry?"

"I was a while ago but now I'm fine."

Resting makes the cold worse, which is why they walked all the way here without pause. Passing places where the trees shaded them from sun made them run if anything. Juryong is impressed that her husband didn't complain about being hungry. In front of the signs, Jeonbin looks this way and that.

"They're supposed to meet us here."

"You didn't set a time?"

"Well, they probably thought we'd arrive later than this."

"Then..." Juryong points down to the two paths ahead. "Which way did they say they'd come down? Wouldn't we run into them if we keep walking?"

Jeonbin shakes his head. "They wouldn't tell me. They need to keep their whereabouts a secret."

"But you must know what region at least?"

"I do..."

"Then which?"

"The right side."

"Shouldn't we walk down that side then?"

"What if we miss them coming by mistake, wouldn't that be a disaster?"

"But just waiting here doing nothing when it's clear where they're coming from is stupid, don't you think?"

Having answered his question with a question, she falls silent. Her frustration is palpable. Mention of stupidity seems to have hurt Jeonbin's feelings as he doesn't speak either.

Their lack of movement makes the cold creep up her hands. Juryong, like on her wedding day, shoves her hands into the opposite sleeves. Rubbing her wrists, she wills her hands to get warm. Her wrists are cold, but her hands are even colder, they're like someone else's hands. The cold and the frustration of having to stay put makes her kick a stone. The stone goes farther than she expects, and she stares at it. Her feet are so frozen that she can't even feel how hard she kicked it.

Jeonbin doesn't look cold at all, he's looking for a spot under the sign to sit down. Is he really going to just wait? In this weather? They'll freeze if they don't move. They could literally freeze—she doesn't want to treat her husband like a fool, but if the sun sets while they're on this road, their lives would be in peril.

And what was this coming to meet them business? Why couldn't they have arranged a proper time to meet? Were they recruiting live fighters or frozen corpses?

"Hey!" Her lips are frozen and her voice hoarse from cold. "I'm going to go down the right-side road. It's not going to help the cause by just sitting here and freezing!"

"What if they come to meet us from the other road?"

"Wouldn't we see them from here if they were coming soon? But we can't!"

Jeonbin is about to answer back but he gives up with a sigh. She thought he was going to admit defeat and go along with her, but he sits down and doesn't move, which annoys her to no end.

Juryong walks down the right-side path like she said she would. But she worries how they're already at odds when they've only just left home. It occurs to her they've never fought like this before. Never had she felt disgruntled by her husband, nor had Jeonbin told her what to do or how to do something. They say a true friend shines through only in times of difficulty—had they never fought simply because things had never been difficult before? The thought weighs on her mind.

How long did she walk? The rumble of an engine and the sound of gravel crunching under wheels wake her from her thoughts. She looks up. A truck is coming in her direction. On a hunch, she jumps into the middle of the road and stops the truck.

"Hey, hey!"

The truck stops right in front of her. The driver's side door opens and a man with a peaceful expression pops his head out. Juryong is quick to speak before he does.

"Do you know a man named Choi Jeonbin?"

He confers with the man sitting in the passenger seat.

Juryong strikes her chest as she shouts again. "I'm Choi Jeonbin's wife! Do you know Choi Jeonbin?"

Finally, the man in the passenger seat suddenly gets wide-eyed and he comes out of the truck.

"It's Jeonbin's wife! I'm Oga, childhood friend of Jeonbin. Do you recognize me?"

Oga, the man with whom she'd occasionally crossed paths with not long after she had moved in with Jeonbin's family. He and Jeonbin had taken night classes together. His name isn't quite familiar and she has seen him only a few times, but running into anyone in a place like this is like running into family.

"Of course I recognize you! Glad to see you again."

Perhaps under the impression their talk will be longer than expected, the man in the driver's seat kills the engine and comes to stand with them in the road. Oga, at first all smiles at this unexpected encounter with someone from home, carefully asks her a question.

"But how... Why are you here alone?"

Juryong realizes Jeonbin had never told them she was coming with him. Neither Oga nor the driver can quite hide their consternation at her presence despite their smiles.

How could he have not told them about me? Did he think I'd abandon him in the middle of our running away? She hides her disappointment with a cheerful answer.

"I was too worried about my husband to let him go on his own, so I followed him all the way out here. Isn't that foolish of me? He's waiting by the sign down the road."

The driver snorts. A sound that irritates Juryong.

"What's so funny? Can't a woman lend a hand for liberation? Isn't that the kind of thinking from an old world?"

The driver laughs even louder at this, so hard that it takes him a moment to recover his breath before answering, waving away her hostility.

"No, no, it's just that you're fierier than most men. I'm glad you're here." He opens the driver side door again and finally introduces himself. "I'm Baek Gwangwoon. Get in. Let's find your husband."

★

The sight of his wife, who had plodded away in a huff, returning on a truck excitedly waving her hand, is quite the surprise for Jeonbin.

Juryong hops off with Oga and happily shouts at him.

"Didn't I tell you that we'd meet them faster if we walked this way?"

Jeonbin gets up with some difficulty, his body stiff with cold. "Yes, my wife, you were right."

Juryong is embarrassed about being smug as she quickly rubs her husband's arms and hands. "You must be so cold, I should've forced you to come with me. It's my fault."

"No, you were right all along, it's me who was stubborn, I'm sorry."

His words make Juryong hug him, Oga and Baek's eyes be damned.

Jeonbin is so cold that Oga decides to ride in the truck bed while Juryong and Jeonbin ride in the middle and passenger seats inside. Even before the engine starts again, Juryong grabs hold of Jeonbin's hand and doesn't let go. Jeonbin leans to the side and whispers in her ear. "I thought you would come back after a little walk."

Juryong also leans toward him and whispers. "Then how happy you must've been when you saw me again."

"The hyungnims must think I'm a fool."

These words stab Juryong in the heart.

She's about to reply that what he just said can't possibly be true when Baek Gwangwoon, his hands on the steering wheel, chides them.

"I don't approve of this whispering. Makes me feel left out."

The couple sit up straight and keep at a distance from one another, but soon the bumpy road gives them a good excuse to lean against each other once more. They must not fall asleep, it'll make them look like they're not alert enough—this is the last thought Juryong has before she falls into a deep, snoring slumber.

4

"We're here. The base of the First Regiment of the Tongeuibu Unified Korea Council."

Juryong quickly wipes away her drool. Outside the windshield, on the side of the dark mountain, are about at least 200 soldiers holding torches aloft.

"Let's go," says Baek Gwangwoon, dispassionately. Oga hops off from the truck bed, opens the passenger-side door. Jeonbin carefully steps out, followed by Juryong who leaps to the ground. Baek drives off somewhere.

"You'll move as part of the First Regiment's Second Squadron," says Oga as he leads the way. "Although you'll be looking at a month of training before seeing any combat... But today is a special day, the general will make a speech and there's a gathering after, it's why I asked you to come on this day."

"So many people," comments Juryong as she notes the almost complete lack of other women.

Oga takes up a torch and guides Juryong and Jeonbin to the Second Squadron line. There are thirty people standing before her, and the diminutive Juryong could only just about make out the top of the rock she assumes the general will make a speech on.

A thunderous applause arises, echoing in the mountains. Their driver, Baek Gwangwoon, gets up on the rock. The shouting and clapping rings in Juryong's ears as she turns to Oga with a question.

"Who is he to get up there?"

"That's General Baek, the leader of the First Regiment of the Tongeuibu."

Jeonbin is even more surprised than Juryong. They hadn't thought to ask him about himself beyond his name.

"Can't hear a damn thing with all the yelling and the stomping," mumbles Juryong, but Jeonbin's eyes are red with tears. Juryong pokes him on the side. "You love that man that much? More than your wife?"

Jeonbin grins and whispers in her ear, "There's something I wish you can do for me, Wife."

"What's that?"

"It's one thing for a married couple to join the Liberation Army together, but being too public about our affections will annoy the others."

"What are you talking about? I'm not going to change."

Instead of an answer, Jeonbin grips her hand. Juryong wants to pout more, but she squeezes back.

The applause and the stomps of the soldiers continue for a long time.

★

Juryong's tasks in the Liberation Army are not very different from what she's used to doing at home.

"You want all this cooked in this tiny little pot?"

They said something about the sixty or so ears of corn being donated from a nearby village as they put down the pile in front of her. When Jeonbin had said women could contribute to liberation as well, she had no idea this was what such contribution would look like.

"If the woman Kang doesn't find a way to do it, we're all going to starve today."

With that, the comrade who'd brought it over leaves her to her own devices. Juryong in other words, is responsible for feeding the mouths of the thirty or so soldiers in the Tongeuibu First Regiment's Second Squad.

Were the few women she had glimpsed on her first day also doing this in their respective divisions? Juryong breaks the corn and stuffs as many of them in the brass pot, but it fits only twenty at most. Maybe making a soup out of the kernels would be better. Using the potlid, she grills a few ears and is soon lost in thought.

At least a month of training, they'd said, but it was hardly that. They were given sticks instead of rifles to practice fighting with bayonets, and after about a week, the sticks were taken away and they were told they would begin combat immediately. But Juryong didn't so much as get to hold a stick. When they gave her barley, she made barley soup. Potatoes, she roasted them. But they hadn't said anything about women not being put into missions, at least.

The way they give her work—figure out a way to do it, or not. And it was this "or not" that makes her want to scream into the mountains. Giving her work that couldn't possibly be done, threatening her by saying they would all starve if she didn't, and when she does figure it out and serve it up, they complain the food is too burned, too bland, too tart, instead of shutting up and eating. And those uniforms they wear against the cold were so dirty she washed them, but they took up whichever washed uniform they liked, leaving Jeonbin with one that's too small to fit him. He looks like an idiot in those too-short sleeves. Not to mention the cold.

And what's more, back home he had slept in later than she, but now he goes out with the other soldiers at dawn and comes back after dark. The two of them sleep clinging to each other to not freeze to death, but there's nothing of the pleasant conversations they used to have. Every night, she looks into his sleeping face. Unlike Juryong, Jeonbin grew up pampered and with plenty, but now her prince has become a mountain man. Living in snow caves is warmer than she expected, but cold seeps up from the ground despite every blanket and rag they put down.

Is there some law that says a liberation army must live in the mountains? Can't they at least retreat from activities a little during the winter? But instead, here they are having climbed through the harsh winter mountains instead of taking the roads to avoid the Japanese, just setting up camp near some who-knows-what village in who-knows-what region. No matter where they settle, their footprints in the snow are bound to give them away, so what's the point of all this, but she is told as long as they don't step too firmly in the snow, the winds would blow away such traces.

"Woman Kang! You are here!"

From the dead trees emerges Baek Gwangwoon.

"Well if it isn't General Baek." He'd made no sound until calling out to her, and Juryong stares at him as if he's a ghost. "What brings you here?"

"Just call me Gwangwoon-ssi. Why are you alone?"

Juryong gestures with her chin at the sacks of corn and the brass pot. Gwangwoon nods, understanding.

"I always say," continues Gwangwoon, "that there are some feats only women are capable of pulling off."

Juryong listlessly looks down on the ground, uninterested. "Huh, like this?"

"I'm not talking about this."

What was he going on about? Juryong looks up at him with suspicion.

Gwangwoon laughs. "You can't tell a lie, can you? Even if you wanted to."

More ridicule. Juryong picks up an ear of corn and starts to prepare it. "Did you see that Jeong or whatever his name is? He dumped this on me and went the way you came."

"I didn't. But you haven't even memorized the names of all your comrades yet?"

"What? Do they even think of me as their comrade?"

Not finding a way to answer this, Gwangwoon sits down next to her. "Let me share the fire with you a bit."

"Fine with me. Us being *comrades* and all."

Gwangwoon laughs again, and he drags the sack of corn in front of her to him. Under Juryong's eye, he takes out a small knife from his pocket. She'd thought of him as a driver, but the way he quietly appeared to her from the mountain just now made her think he was a tiger hunter. What else was in the many pockets of his coat made of animal hide?

"I was looking about for a gathering place, but I came upon something scarier than a tiger. The woman Kang."

"What?" Her surprise makes him laugh, but he doesn't say more.

Like he's reading my mind. Juryong's hands are busy, but she keeps staring at Gwangwoon, who deftly shucks the corn and separates the raw kernels, dropping them into the pot, pretending not to notice her stare.

★

"Are you sleeping?"

It's getting on late at night when someone says this outside of Juryong and Jeonbin's snow cave. Through the opening, they could see a few pairs of feet in leather shoes.

"No, I'm awake," Jeonbin hastily replies as he gets up and begins to crawl out of their cave.

"Not you, Jeonbin, it's your wife."

"What about her?"

"General Baek wants to see her."

The two in the cave look at each other, confused.

Juryong whispers, "Let's go together."

"But he's asking for you."

"No man, not even a general should ask a married woman to come see him in the middle of the night all by herself. Stop talking and just come with me."

The two crawl out of the cave.

Gwangwoon, who's been waiting for them with a burning pine torch that's about to go out in his hand, dismisses the other men. He must have something secretive to say to her. What on earth could he possibly have to say to a nothing of a woman like her? Gwangwoon gives Jeonbin a look that tells him to leave as well, it's like her suspicions were right. Juryong moves closer to Jeonbin, afraid he would actually leave. She tries to hold his hand because why not, but Jeonbin is standing too stiffly for her to do so.

After a moment of hesitation, Gwangwoon gives up and begins to speak.

"Sorry for calling you up in the middle of the night. I have a mission for the woman Kang."

Jeonbin is more surprised than Juryong.

"For my wife?"

"Do you see another woman here?"

Juryong knows the other men make fun of Jeonbin for looking like a woman, because of his youth and pallor. Did Gwangwoon know this? Perhaps he didn't, as this is the first time they're exchanging words since the day they joined the Liberation Army. It bothers Juryong that Gwangwoon's tone might be a bit mocking, but Jeonbin himself doesn't react, so she follows his lead.

"Fine, what's this mission you want me on?"

"We're going to move some things together."

"How is that a mission?"

★

They climb over countless mountains in the night to finally get on a train. Juryong nervously looks down at her stomach. She is disguised as a pregnant woman, and her belly is full of gunpowder and a few disassembled guns. Gwangwoon, sitting beside her, is all smiles for whatever reason. There are a few disguised soldiers about them for protection, but a sense of impending disaster keeps her in a cold sweat.

She never again wants to think about the night before. The crawl up the dark mountain on all fours at times, how she rolled back down the slopes several times. Gwangwoon, stolid, a few steps ahead, had never once held out a hand for her. The first two times she excused because, well, the man seemed in a hurry, but the more times he refused to help her, the more she began to hate him until, out of sheer spite, she kept her close enough to him to step on his heels. The sun was high in the sky by the time they reached their destination. Her disguise barely allowed her to even breathe properly, and she had to hold onto her stomach as they ran to catch their train.

"A real mission this is, don't you think?"

"You can feed this mission to the dogs, I need to use the head."

"Just a little longer. It's not far by train."

Even if he'd allowed her to visit the bathroom, she couldn't have used it because of her stomach. Her body is so heavy she might as well be pregnant after all.

"Was this disguise necessary? If there's going to be this many people with us in the first place, couldn't we have divided the weapons between us? Or go through the mountains like we did last night? How did you do this the last time?"

"On the contrary, moving this many things without attracting attention is very dangerous." Gwangwoon's face turns serious. "If we set a time for the delivery and use a truck, what if we run into a roadside inspection? Trains have inspections, too. And to divide what you're carrying now, we'd need seven men. And traveling the whole way by mountain, would it be possible for a company of men carrying packs to do that without being noticed? It's safer than taking the truck, but what about the time and people it would take if we climbed the whole way?"

Juryong considers what he's saying. So what he means is that as dangerous as this method looks, it's actually the fastest way to do it while using the fewest people.

"Many men would've had to risk their lives for this mission. It is thanks to the woman Kang that our task is as easy as it is now."

His words make her feel proud and ashamed at the same time. Proud that this is indeed a true mission, and ashamed that after making a big fuss about following her husband into the liberation movement, the first thing she had done when finally tasked with actually dangerous work, was to whine to the general out of fear.

"We should now keep silent," he whispers. "We're dressed like Manchurians but talking in Korean, it draws unwanted attention." He pretends to fall asleep.

As he said, the two of them wear Manchurian clothing with their raised collars. She had lived in Gando for several years but never worn such clothes, and they feel strange on her. Juryong rests her hands on her belly and tries to pretend to sleep as well.

When did she doze off? Gwangwoon is shaking her awake.

"We've passed our station," he whispers in her ear.

What remains of Juryong's sleep completely shatters. "And none of you noticed? What was everyone doing?"

"We passed our station because we never stopped. The train kept going."

There is only one reason a train would pass a station: orders from the Japanese police.

"Why would they give such an order?"

"Who knows. Maybe they spent too much time in the station before, or someone important is waiting in the station after."

"Is that common?"

"I'm just thinking. I don't think it's that common. Or perhaps…"

"Perhaps?"

"They started searching the train after judging someone suspicious was on it, but they haven't finished with their search yet."

Fear grips her spine. Juryong turns her frightened eyes to her belly.

"What should we do?"

"A moment… Let me think."

Juryong's eyes dart this way and that. Their comrades pretending to be strangers avoid each other's gaze but look worried as they cross and uncross their legs and fiddle with their hands. Her eyes settle on her belly once more. The belly that looks pregnant but is actually fake and full of contraband.

A sudden idea.

"Ah… ah ah…"

Juryong wraps her arms around her belly and moans. Gwangwoon turns to her in surprise and then, with a brief glance of understanding, speaks loudly in Manchurian. Juryong moans, loud enough to drown out his voice.

"Argh! Argh!"

Not knowing a word of Manchurian, Juryong is glad that the language of women about to give birth consists of universal moans and groans. Someone goes to another car and brings a policeman. He has the Japanese flag on his sleeve. Just as Gwang-woon had suspected, they had been searching the train.

The policeman doesn't give in easily. He instructs some of the passengers to move to a different car. He seems to look for a doctor on the train. What if she gets caught? Not only would they lose their goods, but all sorts of hardships would await them in prison. Would they ever get off this train? Forget the train, would she ever get herself to an outhouse? She feels a strong urge to urinate, enough to stomp her feet if she didn't have this disguise—

Urinate?

Juryong screws her eyes shut and lets loose some urine.

Please be fooled. Please be fooled.

She grabs Gwangwoon's sleeve and points downward. Gwangwoon, who is nearing panic, looks where she is pointing, and startled, starts arguing loudly with the policeman. A daring move, but, right now, Juryong is too anxious to admire him for it.

What if the smell makes him realize it's not my water having broken?

The shame inflames her face and tears well up in her eyes. The people giving her curious glances instantly look away. An awkward mood descends. Daunted, the policeman leaves.

Soon, the train slows to a stop.

It's a wasteland outside.

Gwangwoon carefully helps her off the train. Their compatriots who are pretending not to be their compatriots stay on the train as it pulls away.

The freezing wind seeps through Juryong's soaked crotch. Gwangwoon turns his back as Juryong takes off her burden. Juryong changes clothes and begins to walk. A long while after, Gwangwoon catches up to her.

"I don't know what to say."

"Then say nothing."

"I owe you a great debt."

"Not at all."

"We just need to make it to the station, our comrades will be there. The station is—"

"Please, stop talking to me."

★

"Comrades! Tomorrow, our great day finally arrives!"

Thirty or so soldiers stand in a circle, and Gwangwoon raises his voice so they all can hear.

"For half of you, this will be your first mission since joining the Tongeuibu. Congratulations."

He gestures to stop them from applauding. Jeonbin is among those who've raised their hands to clap. As he awkwardly lowers his hands, Juryong looks upon him with sympathy. Jeonbin stands across from her, and she's to the right of General Baek.

"But there is one among you who has already contributed greatly to tomorrow's mission." Gwangwoon pushes Juryong forward. Surprised, Juryong steps into the circle.

"This is our comrade Kang Juryong who has transported many of the weapons that will make our task tomorrow possible."

Gwangwoon is the first to clap at his own words. The soldiers, glancing at each other, begin to clap as well. Juryong feels something surge inside her and she bows her head. She hears a small voice behind her.

"Raise your head."

She does. She sees Jeonbin's face. He looks proud and also envious. An expression she has never seen on him before. The pride she feels turns to shame as she remembers she'd urinated in public. When the applause starts to diminish, she takes it as her cue to hastily step back out of the circle.

Gwangwoon proceeds to outline the strategy and hand down detailed orders. They are to lie in wait in the environs of their targeted building until the night comes and arm themselves just as the sun comes down before their attack. Juryong takes hold of Jeonbin's hand as they return to their snow cave they dug together.

Jeonbin, who normally gives his arm for a pillow to her when they sleep, has his back to her on this night. Odd. Juryong tickles his back. Jeonbin doesn't move at all.

"Did something happen while I was gone?"

"Nothing happened."

"Then what's wrong?"

He hems and haws at first. Carefully, he says, "I heard something about you and the General."

Juryong's tickling hands become still. "Heard what?" Did news of her urinating spread through the encampment? But Baek wasn't such a gossip, surely?

"That you pretended to be married."

Ah, so you do have the will to fight after all. Juryong suppresses a grin as she hugs him from behind.

"What nonsense, when my real husband is right here?"

Jeonbin turns and looks at her. His large, cold hands gently cup her face and make her heart ache.

"I don't know. I'm proud that you've accomplished a big mission, but I keep thinking I'm becoming lesser in comparison."

Juryong wants to confess, too, that whenever he left her behind in the village for his reconnaissance trips or whatever with his comrades, she'd felt the same. That she knew very well what it felt like to become lesser. But if she says this now, she really will become lesser—an admission she can do nothing without her husband. Juryong doesn't want to become such a person, aside from her selfish desire for Jeonbin to be someone who can't do anything without her. So Juryong takes a different tack.

"Aren't my accomplishments yours, in the end?"

Jeonbin scoffs, but his smile indicates he isn't in complete disagreement.

"If I hadn't insisted on following you into the movement, what mission could I have accomplished? So my accomplishment is also my husband's, isn't it?"

Not what she wanted to say at all, but not untrue, either. She has no desire to take sole credit and let her name be known throughout the land. Just like Jeonbin had once said, the reason she wants liberation is for the happiness of the one she married.

She loves him and wants him to live in a liberated country.

5

"You're shaking?"

"Of course I'm shaking in this winter."

Juryong's rejoinder is rude, but Jeonbin hugs her shoulders in response. She wasn't really cold, but his hug felt too good to object to.

"My legs keep falling asleep."

"You've got to stand it. The others will make fun of you."

From sunup to sundown, an entire day, they've been waiting in ambush near the Ilshim office building, the place Jeonbin and some other comrades had spent the last several days searching for and observing.

According to what they know, the office is called Ilshim—Japanese Mind—in the spirit of loyalty to their colonial subjugator. It is a chamber of commerce for Koreans, but it lends money to the Japanese military and Japanese companies in Manchuria while charging exploitative interest rates to Koreans who have been forcibly relocated to the region, a collaborationist entity that has accumulated much capital through corrupt means. On the surface, it's a space where rich old men play go and bring in women and drink, a recreation center. But the members do not go there solely for recreation. They are there every day to ensure the safe is not broken into and to keep an eye on each other.

The goal today is to break into the safe.

"Doesn't that make us robbers?"

When Juryong blurted out this passing thought, she was met with glares all around. Glares that said, how dare she compare the just activities of the Liberation Army to robbery? Even Jeonbin poked her in the ribs, which made her pout at him.

"The woman Kang should have one, too."

It was the first time she had ever held a gun. Carrying them in a pouch over her belly had been nauseating enough, but holding one in her hand makes her break into a cold sweat. It is likely she will never have to pull the trigger. That's probably why Gwang-hoon had given her a gun, no doubt, just to experience it. To use this as a chance to become familiar with holding one in her hand.

But there is still the danger of any security measures all their reconnaissance might have missed, which is why they each need to hold a firearm in case of a confrontation with the Chinese police or Japanese military. Juryong, more than anyone else, hopes it never comes to that. She's learned how to shoot the gun, but she's deathly afraid of making a mistake in the event of an actual gunfight.

The reconnaissance report said there were two or three guards on duty at any time, and two or three ought to be easy enough to overpower. What tightwads, though. All that money and that's all the security they have? Do they know they'd saved all that money on guards just to get it stolen from them? Juryong assuages her boredom by worrying over other people's money. And also worrying that having sat crouched for so long in the cold, her legs would refuse to move when the signal came through to attack.

★

The Manchurian winter night descends upon them like an ambush. Pedestrians vanish with the setting sun, but they wait until proper darkness before making their move. A more seasoned unit of five enters first and the rest follow in separate units. The first rings a bell to summon the guards, overpowers them, and signals the other units to follow. Juryong, dragging her sleeping legs, trails along Jeonbin. Another unit of seven takes the lookout outside. Gwangwoon is set to drive up with the truck that will haul away the spoils.

The building has three levels including the basement. Juryong casts a glance at the expertly tied up guards as she follows Jeonbin through the corridor. Juryong's unit is in charge of the first-floor office, another unit the second floor, and a third searches the basement.

The first-floor office is spacious and luxurious. Three desks and several steel cabinets, leather couches and chairs that could seat about seven or eight arranged in a circle. They pry open the cabinets with a crowbar and stuff whatever they could grab into their sacks. Stealing reams of loan contracts to set on fire later is another part of the mission. Juryong is in charge of the desk. She grabs the drawers and pulls them out completely, shaking their contents into her sack. Official seals made of ivory and jade clack against each other as they drop. A big lump of something in the bottom drawer turns out to be a toad-shaped gold ingot. Money, money, so much money.

She kneels to reach deeper into the desk when she notices a small, old man crouched under the desk. The inside of her head goes white.

"What, what are you bastards doing?" The old man hisses the words like a snake, low enough that only Juryong can hear. There's a second of hesitation as Juryong adjusts the grip on her sack and gun, enough time for the old man to leap toward the wall where a katana blade hangs and unsheathe the sword—he moves so quickly it's hard to believe he's not younger than he is. Normally a gun would trump a sword, but the old man is so near that Juryong freezes in terror.

Another member of her unit finally sees the situation and runs toward them, gun drawn. The old man has seen all his money being stolen in front of him, he fears nothing. Screaming like a beast, he raises his sword. The blade seems to move strangely slow in the dim light, but Juryong's body refuses to move away. The blade smashes against something, creating sparks and a loud noise—her compatriot had blocked the sword with his gun. Finally, Jeonbin and the others notice what's going on and turn toward them. They had all put their guns down to rifle through the cabinets, they don't know what to do.

The arm of her compatriot warding off the sword begins to tremble.

"Shoot him, quickly!" he says through gritted teeth to Juryong. Her finger hovers over the trigger but she can't pull it. The blade begins to slip and slices the younger man's arm and shoulder. Juryong closes her eyes.

A deafening gunshot.

She opens her eyes. How could there be a gunshot, when she didn't pull the trigger?

Jeongga, from one of the other units, stands in the doorway. Smoke issues from the barrel of the gun in his hands. The old man, sprawled on the floor, jerks a bit before going still. A stream of urine comes out of him. It mixes with his flowing blood. Not knowing how to think or feel, Juryong takes a step back from the encroaching piss and blood.

Jeongga is expressionless. "Let's get out of here."

Gwangwoon's truck stands by the door. They load their full-to-bursting sacks, the safe, and their injured compatriot. The truck quickly drives off, and the rest, as planned, scatter into the night, running as far away as possible before gathering once more in two hours. Juryong looks about her in the dark before following Jeonbin. He runs so fast she can barely keep up.

It begins to snow. Her heart is about to explode.

★

Not knowing the geography very well, Juryong wanders and wanders before arriving at the rendezvous point last. No one points a finger at her as such, but Juryong can't ignore the cold shoulder she's getting from the men.

"A great success, this mission. Comrades, you did well."

Gwangwoon praises the airtight plan, the thorough reconnaissance, and the excellent execution before bidding everyone to applaud. Even as she claps, Juryong cannot stop her face from turning bright red with guilt and shame.

"I hope our new comrades do not take mistakes too much to heart. Mistakes happen often, what matters is that we succeeded in our mission. Even if we had failed, it is not a thing you should fault yourself for. Mistakes that bring down a whole mission can only be committed by higher-ups. We would never assign new comrades a task so important that it brings down the mission if they fail."

It sounds like he's deliberately speaking about her, which makes her bow her head even lower.

Gwangwoon seems perturbed. "I said that so you would all relax. Why is no one relaxing?"

The comrades look at each other before forcing a smile on their lips. The forced smiles look so ridiculous that they start pointing at each other and breaking into genuine laughter.

Jeonbin, who had been standing away from her, comes up to her amidst the laughter. "Wife," he whispers, "you suffered a lot today."

"My husband suffered more."

Carefully looking around at the other men, he takes hold of her hand.

"It's like what the general said, don't take what happened to-day too much to heart."

"Trying not to. But can't help it."

Jeonbin grips her hand firmly. "I'm sure of it now. That it was good you came with me. If we work together, liberation will come twice as fast. I want to keep doing this until the day we both return to our liberated country. I want to see the place my wife is from."

She nods in answer but still can't shake her complicated feelings. It's joyful to see her handsome husband happy, but how exactly does robbing a rich collaborationist organization contribute to the cause of liberation? Surely the goods will be used to buy provisions and weapons or be divided among the higher-ups, but it's still not something she can understand on her own.

"It's good to see you smile," she says as she pets the back of his head.

"Might I have a word with our comrade, the woman Kang?"

It's Gwangwoon. Juryong and Jeonbin look at each other, wondering what is going on.

Is he going to ask me to pose as a pregnant woman again?

Gwangwoon takes her to a clearing a little off to the side, out of earshot of the others, and asks her for her thoughts on the mission. Jeongga, who acts as second in command, seems to have told Gwangwoon what had happened that night.

"I don't know, Sir, I've heard many times these were evil men, but to shoot someone who is right in front of me made my heart tremble so, I thought I would die first."

Gwangwoon doesn't say anything. He is listening, patient.

"The old man when he was shot, he pissed himself. I don't

know if he did it before or after the bullet. But it made me think, oh, he is a man, not a demon or a ghost but a man, that's what I was thinking. Like me pissing myself on the other mission." Her voice gets quieter and quieter. "Maybe because I'm just a woman... Maybe a woman just can't help it... Maybe I should've stuck to the cauldrons in the kitchen and done nothing else..."

Furious, Gwangwoon grabs her shoulders. "You mustn't say that to yourself. If you call yourself a kitchen wench, you'll be treated like one, but if you act like a Liberation Army soldier, you'll be treated like a warrior!"

His words infuriate her. "But it's the comrades who made me into a kitchen wench first!"

Gwangwoon doesn't say anything to that. Juryong, embarrassed at her outburst, also falls silent.

Finally, Gwangwoon speaks.

"When you have trouble understanding what your deeds mean to your country, think of your comrade, the person standing next to you."

Juryong thinks of the new comrade who had become injured because of her. The man who would be fine now had she pulled the trigger. He had hurt himself because he'd cared more about saving her than his own life. Not because he considered Juryong beneath him, like she said, but because she was his comrade and cared about her.

If they truly think of me as their comrade like that, then I shall lay down my life for them as well.

Instead of saying this out loud, she nods. For now, it is probably a good idea to keep all the noisome questions in her mind to herself. The thought cools her head and heart.

"What did the general say?" asks Jeonbin when she crawls into their snow cave to join him. Juryong only smiles wanly.

★

From then on, Juryong asks to be put on watch duty at base during missions. No one objects to this. Whether it's because they respect her wishes or they think she's no help during missions, she doesn't care.

The new comrades including Jeonbin and Juryong soon come to realize that Gwangwoon had congratulated them on their first mission being a success because it had been precisely that. On the missions that follow, many become seriously injured or even killed by the Japanese army.

Over the next two changes in seasons, the thirty-strong company dwindles to about twenty. There are members who are too injured to continue their activities, those who passed away, and some who desert them. There is no way to hold on to those who have endured the cold winter in the mountains only to long for their idle fields come spring. But the resentment is inevitable. Morale is never lower than when someone leaves, even more so than when a comrade is injured or killed.

Even Jeonbin, filled with boyish adventure and patriotic zeal in his first mission, has begun to lose the light in his eyes. It's Juryong who hasn't been disappointed in any high expectations, as her intentions from the start were merely to follow her husband wherever he goes.

Gwangwoon is busy but seems particularly concerned with the goings on of Second Squadron of which Jeonbin and Juryong are a part. It's how he treats Juryong, especially, that's notable. He always calls her up before and after a mission to discuss things, encourages her when she makes mistakes, and if there is the slightest task she excels at, he praises her in front of everyone else. Juryong feels uncomfortable with the special attention at first but comes to depend on it more and more. Her frustrations with the other men who act like they don't see or hear her disappears into thin air with him. Gangwon feels like the older brother Juryong has never had, and Gwangwoon himself seems to think of her as an aching finger worthy of notice. He does seem to pay extra attention to those comrades who seem in danger of desertion. And his belief in the importance of women in the liberation movement is likely another reason he takes such care with her.

The others seemed to think differently.

They are mostly of western Gando extraction, but a few of them are from faraway Korea. The reason they have joined the Tongeuibu in Gando instead of a liberation movement closer to them is because of their admiration for General Baek Gwangwoon. Jeonbin is the same. Juryong still remembers how surprised and moved Jeonbin was when he realized their driver was none other than the legendary general.

No wonder this awkward woman fighter inspires such ire for commandeering so much of the general's attention. Juryong isn't unaware of this. But isn't it beyond the pale for them to whisper and giggle whenever she's summoned by the general? Even if she were to forgive that, the real problem is that Jeonbin can't seem to disregard their jeering.

Juryong is an ordinary woman who was taught from an early age that the greatest virtue a woman can aspire to is to care for her parents and submit to her husband. To point fingers at herself and Gwangwoon is to soil her reputation and to insult her husband who stands there with his eyes wide open in view of all that goes on. Juryong is aware of her so-called comrades slandering her behind her back. No one is more sensitive to their finger-pointing than she is. Even as she wonders which of the bastards she can grab by the scruff of the neck and make an example out of, what really makes her shake her head at herself is Jeonbin, who is no doubt completely unaware of how she feels. What if she had come to fisticuffs with a comrade and she were banished? They were not children playing at soldiers, there were real rules they needed to follow, a hierarchy. Even if she were to avoid banishment, it would greatly dishonor Jeonbin. So the best she can do for now is smile like a fool.

★

A day of excellent luck. During a survey of the people of a nearby village, they are gifted a few bottles of barley wine. Jeongga and some other men catch pheasants and rabbits, and while the sun is still up, they cook the meat and pour the wine, having a modest feast. The only regret is that Gwangwoon isn't present at this rare festivity, but Juryong knows that to comment would only occasion suspicion, so she keeps silent.

The wine reddens the faces of the men. One of the tipsy men pats the spot next to where he sits and calls for Juryong.

"The woman Kang, my comrade Kang. Come sit next to me."

"Don't want to." She adds a smile to her refusal. The drunk men laugh as one. But it doesn't end there.

"What, I'm not a man in your eyes because I'm no general?"

It's like the party has been doused with icy water. Juryong jumps to her feet, glares at him like she's about to kill him, then storms off. Jeonbin follows.

She's about to walk right off the mountain when Jeonbin grabs her shoulder. "Let go!" She pushes him away.

Jeonbin falls down to the ground. Juryong, incensed as she is, covers her mouth in shock at what she's done.

But Jeonbin speaks as if nothing just happened. "How would our comrades feel if you just run off like that?"

"Comrades? You care about how they feel more than me?"

Jeonbin sighs. "He's drunk and said something stupid. If you just go off like that, what would that do for morale?"

"Well, look at my fancy husband. Such a big boy that he doesn't even bat an eyelid at an insult upon his wife's honor?"

Fierce anger cuts through Jeonbin's glare. Juryong has never seen him like this.

"Do you know what the men say? That I'm a little bastard who carries the general's washbasin. But have I said a single word that you go around with the general all the time?"

This angers her so much she strikes her own chest. "What did you just say?"

"I'm not done yet. There's more they say. That your skirt is so wide it covers two men and then some."

The cold mountain wind swirls around them as it passes.

"And you just stood there listening to them?" Her voice is low. Jeonbin begins to shed tears as big as pearls.

"What else can I do? I dreamed of fighting in the movement for so long. If I made a fuss and was kicked out, would that make my wife happy? Should I get mad and shoot the man who says it?"

"I would've. If someone talked about my husband like that, I would've made a bullet hole in him."

They stare at each other without a word for a while. Some other time, she would've pitied his tears and brought him into a hug. But not today.

Jeonbin must've had his own hardships. To smile away the insults to his wife in the name of unity wouldn't have been easy. But who cared about that kind of unity? If this unity couldn't be maintained without insult to a woman or a young man, wouldn't it be a hundred times better without it? When will these jokers learn that no matter how much they pose, they'll never be even half the man as General Baek?

Juryong sighs as she makes an apology she doesn't mean. "Sorry I made such a fuss. Let's go back up."

"I don't want you to."

Juryong can't believe her ears. "You don't want me to?"

"Yeah. I don't want you to." His eyes fill with tears.

You fool. You just chose a bunch of men who don't respect you over your wife who would lay her life down for you. Do you think that's patriotism? My heart will never mend over this. You have just lost me forever, do you know that?

But she doesn't speak these thoughts. Instead, she grits her teeth and says in a low voice, "Fine. I won't bother you then. Let's go back up."

Jeonbin shakes his head and looks her directly in the eye. "You go back. Go back home."

Juryong stares at her husband's tear-stained face and turns away from him.

"If that's what you want. I'm going home."

She leaves him behind on the mountain.

6

Who knows how she made it back to her village.

While there was no cold that cut to the bone like when she'd left, each step she took laid a layer of hurt over her heart, so much so the tears came every night. Travelers on the road spat at her as she cried and walked. Unlucky bitch.

She shouldn't have left when he told her to. She should've grabbed onto his ankle and begged him to let her stay.

She struck her chest in frustration and tore at her hair but kept walking and walking. Who knew if Jeonbin would've forgiven her had she turned back. But even if she were to do so, the regiment had probably moved on and there would be no way to find him. She couldn't go back.

The farther she got, the fainter her resentment became and the more she worried over her young husband—how would he survive his harsh path? The worry made her cry and cry. The argument they parted on evaporated. If she had stayed, the argument would've been a stain on their marriage. But once he had said worse, the argument seemed trivial in comparison.

My husband isn't dead, is it worth all these tears?

Hesitant before the entrance to her in-laws' village, she turns instead toward her parents' home. It's more than fifteen li away.

She's come a hundred li, what's another fifteen? She can't bear to see her in-laws' faces and Jeonbin may have meant their separation to be permanent, which makes her reluctant to walk into her in-laws' on her own two feet.

★

As the shadows lengthen and she steps into the courtyard, her mother tosses aside what she was doing and runs outside. Despite the state of Juryong's clothes and the messy nest of her hair, her mother recognizes her on sight.

"You silly girl, you silly little girl, where were you all this time, how could you come back in this state," her mother shouts as she hits Juryong's back and chest before her tears burst. Juryong cries along with her. Not because her mother's half-hearted blows hurt but because they make it real to her that her mother, whose face appeared so many times in her dreams, is truly there.

Her father, who had looked out when he heard the noise, also runs out into the courtyard in his bare feet.

"What happened? Tell us what happened, where did you leave your husband? Did he cast you out? Did your husband go to his home and send you here?"

"No, not that. Don't ask me anymore."

Displeased, her father clears his throat and returns to his room. Juryong knows this is the extent to his expression of relief on her return, but it still hurts to tears.

"I'll heat water for you, wash up and go to your room." Her mother gently pats her cheek. "Look at the state of your face..." She wipes away tears.

"Mother..."

"What?"

"I know I'm in a state but please give me a hug."

Mother and daughter throw themselves into an embrace and cry like animals. Normally, her father would say it's unlucky for a girl's cries to be heard all the way outside a home, but even he stays silent. Her young brother comes to the courtyard hearing them and realizes his sister has come home—he throws himself at her and cries along with them.

Oh, oh, I really am back home now.

The thought drowns out her worries over her husband for a moment.

★

From the very next day, Juryong falls back into chores like she has never left the house. Her hands must be busied if she's to drown out her worries.

She burns all of her clothes. Like most Korean families forcibly relocated to Gando, Juryong's family faced many hardships in this new land. Juryong is afraid she might carry some disease into the house from all her time outside, or whether some bloodstain would invite questions from her mother. She decides to burn her whole past in the fire. It is the smallest and yet most important decision she can make about her past now. To shut up about it.

Her story about her time away is that she and Jeonbin were in the goldmines. There were rumors of young people trying their luck there, which is a safer story than the truth, which can get her arrested and their families persecuted. Even this explanation came only when her mother persisted in her demands for an explanation as to their prolonged absence.

Rumors of her reappearance spread, and her husband's family sent word that all would be forgiven if she returns.

It's not just her news that reaches them, she hears about what happened with her in-laws as well. The day Juryong and

Jeonbin disappeared, the grandmother flew into such a rage that a stroke and senility struck at the same time, with Juryong's mother-in-law and sister-in-law stuck with the fallout. She pitied them but had no desire to return to that life. Unless Jeonbin returned himself.

Every dawn, Juryong wakes up in a sweat.

The last time she saw him, Jeonbin hadn't told her to go wait for him at home. He'd never promised he'd see her again.

He just told her to go back. Like she was too bothersome.

His harshness, his terrible words make Juryong's sleep lighter and lighter. Jeonbin appears in her dreams, appears outside of them, too. Juryong becomes thinner, gaunter, and her hallucinations grow that much clearer, substantial.

She dares not speak of these things either.

★

As it has in years past, fall comes early. It also leaves early. Winter rules the year.

In the freeze, Juryong's whole family sleeps together in the jeongjugan, lying as close to the oven as they can. Memories of her marriage and the independence fighters seem as distant as her childhood. Her groom's soft and lovely face is but a dream now. And no news of Jeonbin comes with the approaching spring.

The harshness of Gando's long winters is no longer a surprise to Juryong. All she feels in the midst of surviving one day after the other is the phantom warmth of a new season.

To not wait is the only way to endure waiting. That's how Juryong survives.

It's on another cold evening, when the sun has set and the dark is descending on another day of not waiting, when news finally arrives.

Oga, Jeonbin's old friend from Dongri, bursts through her door. Even before she sees the shadow on his face, Juryong senses the news he brings is bad.

"Jeonbin is dying!"

Oga says this before Juryong could even ask, "What are you doing here? How are you?" The other folks, startled at a strange man at their door, hear Jeonbin's name and immediately understand.

"Dying... What exactly do you mean? What happened to him?"

"I ask you to come see for yourself."

"But where is he? Back in Dongri?"

"Yuhahyun."

At least a hundred li from where they are. The color fades from Juryong's face as she stands up and turns to her family, who are sitting there with dropped jaws.

"I don't need to pack much. Lead the way."

The land outside is frozen over, and Juryong imagines Oga climbing over the icy mountains as he walked the hundred li to their house and now another hundred li back.

"You must be tired. I am so sorry for all of this."

"Not at all. I hitched a wagon ride for part of my way here."

Oga's face is briefly illuminated by his torch. The visibly deep creases of worry and strife in his visage silence any further inquiries Juryong has about her husband. She forgets thoughts of fatigue, her fear of mountain beasts. There's only that dreadful sense she's walking in place for hours in the dark.

It is dawn when Juryong and Oga pass a signpost for Yuhahyun.

Five more li from the signpost brings them to a tiny fenceless house far out from the town proper. Oga quickens his steps and slips inside. Juryong, hesitating as she gathers her courage, follows him.

"Look, Jeonbin! She's here, the woman Kang is here. Do you hear me?"

There are two other people in the room. One is a stranger Juryong surmises is the cottage owner. The other is, as Oga said, Jeonbin.

The husband she had longed to see lies whimpering, his eyes rolled back.

So stricken she is by the sight, Juryong collapses to her knees. Never would she have guessed this is how they would be reunited.

"Husband, your wife is here. Me, Juryong. Please, open your eyes."

The owner of the house brushes away Juryong's hands.

"You mustn't shake him so, he is not well!"

Jeonbin is indeed breathing shallow and fast. How could he be so sick, what is his sickness, what was everyone doing that they let him get to this state—Juryong clenches her teeth against the countless retorts inside her. Plenty of time for tears after her husband gets better. Suppressing all other questions, she manages to start with the most important.

"Is he... Is he eating?"

Oga answers, "We can sit him up and give him rice gruel, but he might choke on it."

Juryong pulls her dagger from its sheath. Dagger though it was, the blade is so dull she needs to press it hard against her left ring finger. A bead of blood flows down her hand. Realizing what she's doing, Oga and the cottage owner try to take her knife from her.

"Let go of me!"

"What are you doing? You must keep your head—"

"Let go!"

Juryong pushes them away. A few precious drops of blood fall on the floor. Afraid to lose any more, she holds her right hand underneath the wound and brings the flow to her husband's lips, slipping her ring finger into his mouth.

Jeonbin, unable to swallow, lets the blood flow out the corner of his lips.

Juryong gently takes hold of Jeonbin's chin. She widens Jeonbin's lips with her inserted finger and eases it in deeper. She wipes away the spilled blood around his mouth. The blood no longer flows out.

"He's taking it in. He's taking it in!"

The landlord, crouching down with hands on knees, peers into Jeonbin's face and shouts this with relief. "He's taking it in. He's taking it in." The words sound far away to Juryong, or like they're coming from beyond some wall. She is completely focused on her bleeding finger. This man is alive. The inside of his mouth is still warm. Her wound on her finger is more sensitive to the heat. She detects another change: Jeonbin's throat is moving, she feels him sucking her finger.

"My husband, my husband! Can you hear me!"

With her finger in his mouth, she can't move much, but her voice rises as she calls for her husband. Jeonbin's half-open eyes that had been regarding the ceiling suddenly blink and open wider. It can't be said his eyes shine with health, but it is enough to make the people surrounding him shout with joy.

"My dear."

Jeonbin mumbles this with Juryong's finger in his mouth. Juryong takes her hand away and covers her still bleeding left hand with her right. The house owner and Oga are beside themselves.

"He's alive! He's alive."

"Jeonbin! Can you hear me? Comrade Juryong saved your life! She saved you!"

Juryong only crouches by Jeonbin's head, her hands clasped before her.

"My dear... why... why are you wounded?"

Juryong sees Jeonbin is looking at her bleeding finger. Silence descends. The house owner and Oga make their excuses to leave the room, the latter saying he will let others know the good news, leaving the two of them alone.

"Why are you here?"

"I walked."

"That's not what I asked."

Unwell as he is, and only moments ago unconscious from sickness, Jeonbin gives out a feeble laugh. How could he laugh in a moment like this?

"I have some questions myself," she says.

"What are they?"

"Did you cast me out all alone just to get to this pitiful state?"

Jeonbin has no answer to that. Juryong puts the finger she'd put in her husband's mouth into her own. Drinking her own blood, she cries silently.

Oga borrows a horse and rides away. Only the house owner comes to look after Jeonbin and Juryong. Apologizing for the lack of food, as reserves always ran low in early spring, the owner leaves behind some steamed sweet potatoes and doesn't return.

The sweet potatoes grow completely cold and almost reharden; Juryong has no appetite and refuses to touch them. She is afraid Jeonbin won't wake up every time he falls asleep, but the thought that he needs to sleep to recover makes her refrain from waking him. And while he slumbers, she goes to the toilet and rekindles the fire and heats up water to wipe her husband's sweat and clean herself. Such things, the kind of things one does to survive and because one has survived, makes her feel guilty whenever she sees her husband's face.

The house is on a mountain where night descends quickly. Jeonbin, who had been sleeping uneasily with shallow breaths, suddenly utters a long sentence as if he had never fallen unconscious.

"With me lying here and you sitting down, it makes me think of when we got married."

Juryong stirs herself from sleep. "A foolish thing to say to me now."

"Back then you were lying down and I sitting, and you kept asking me to come in underneath the covers."

"Yes, that's true."

"Come in here."

"No."

"Why, you don't like it that your groom is so young?"

"No."

"You think I'm ugly?"

"How dare you say you're ugly."

"Then come inside."

Not taking off her tunic or skirt, Juryong dives in underneath the covers. Jeonbin can't move for his sickness, which means half her body lies outside the bedding.

The married couple lie side by side and look up to the ceiling. The soft sound of Jeonbin's breathing rustles in Juryong's ear. Fearing he may lose consciousness again, Juryong asks him a question.

"What are you thinking?"

"Nothing. What are you thinking, my wife?"

Those few words make Jeonbin short of breath. Juryong rolls onto her side toward him.

"Whether if… if I had just let you go on your own, things would have been better."

"What are you talking about?"

"If I had been like other women and waited with your family for you… waited until I heard news from you…"

"Then you would've become an old woman, still waiting to hear the news that I was long dead."

"Don't talk about dying. That's bad luck."

Despite her protest, she knows. He is not going to get better. Whether it was to happen today or tomorrow, the thought of her young husband's imminent death draws an icy line through her thoughts. The pale white moonlight glows through the paper window and shines on Jeonbin's lips. Moving those lips, Jeonbin speaks again.

"I'm glad my wife did what she did."

Juryong can't answer right away. How could he say such a thing? When he has already left her once? When he is about to leave her for good, how could he say such a loving thing? He never should've taken her as his bride. She never should've given him her love. She should've spurned him on their wedding night. If she'd known this were to happen... Juryong reaches out and touches Jeonbin's face.

"I'm glad you're my husband, too."

As soon as she says this, Juryong senses a strange silence. The slight movements of Jeonbin's chin ceases. His shallow breath scattering into the darkness is no more. Juryong bolts upright into a sitting position and grips his arm.

She puts an ear to every place where there should be a pulse. His body is warm, but there is no breathing. No beating of the heart.

In the moonlight, Juryong rummages through her things.

Finding the needle she had pierced into her wrapping cloth, she pricks Jeonbin's body with it all over. Her hands shake so much she inadvertently plunges an inch of the needle into him, but Jeonbin doesn't move. Only then can she admit it. Jeonbin is dead. The friend she thought she'd have for the rest of her life is gone.

Juryong goes back to where she had lain before and tries to go to sleep. She is determined to take in all of his warmth into her own body before he cools for good.

She must've dozed off because she wakes at the sound of footsteps. Daylight outside. When she opens the door, she sees the yard is full of the men of the Second Squadron under the command of Baek Gwangwoon. Oga approaches eagerly but she raises her hand to halt him.

"You've come to a funeral," she says in a low voice.

Silence falls like cold rain on the gathered.

"Please come in and say goodbye to my husband." She throws open the door. The smell of death that had begun to gather in the room mixes with the cold spring air.

★

With the help of the men, she buries Jeonbin. The ground is frozen and unreceptive to spades at first, but the men take turns until a respectably sized hole is dug, large enough for one young man to be buried. Juryong, sleeves rolled, pitches in with the dig.

She doesn't blink once as they lower her husband into the hole, no coffin, just wrapped in a makeshift shroud. What she wants is to jump into the hole, lay herself next to him, and cry and scream. But she doesn't have any strength left in her. Her eyes are open, but she feels like she's already fainted.

Someone finds out the train time to Tonghwahyeon, and she rides it back. She gets off and walks the rest of the way, all fifteen li. Jeonbin's village appears on the horizon.

Her in-laws greet her with feigned gladness. Even feigned, it makes her uncomfortable. The sick old grandmother, the household clearly in need of more hands. They no doubt expect the new bride to jump in with the work until her husband returns.

Not knowing said new bride had come to give them news that their son would never come back.

Her mother-in-law drags her to see the grandmother. She stinks where she lies, and Juryong doesn't know what to say. Her mother-in-law pokes Juryong's side.

"Where are your manners? Say hello to her!"

Juryong takes a deep breath, kneels before the old woman, and intones, "Your grandson has died."

Everyone in the room freezes. The grandmother, long insensate, says nothing. The mother-in-law collapses onto the floor.

"What, what did you just say?"

"Grandmother, your second grandson, Choi Jeonbin, has died," Juryong says.

Her mother-in-law rubs her chest as if her heart is about to explode. "You said he was in the gold mines? That he would come back rich?"

She had believed the lie Juryong had told. Juryong wished she could believe it, too. That the husband who died yesterday was fake, and the real Choi Jeonbin was in the gold mines. But her finger still aches from having fed her blood to him. The side, she had held against his dead body all night, was still cold. There is no way she can fool herself—Jeonbin is dead.

"What gold mine can there possibly be? He fought for liberation, got sick, and died. I'd gone with him at first and he made me return, so I—"

Before she can finish, stars appear. Her mother-in-law has slapped her in the face.

"What did you just say?"

Blows rain down on Juryong. She withstands them. She lets her mother-in-law hit whatever she wants to hit.

"I stuck him with a wife so he'd stop with that foolishness, but two leave and only one comes back? How dare you!" She stops shaking Juryong's shoulders and and starts to plead with her instead. "Say it's a lie. Say you said it because you hate your mother-in-law, you wanted to see me lose my mind. Say it. Say it's a lie!"

Juryong unwraps the bundle she brought with her and shows her mother-in-law the last possessions of her son. After much pounding of her own chest and lamentations, she grabs Juryong by the hair and drags her out into the courtyard.

"You murderous bitch! I can kill you ten times and it wouldn't be enough!"

Juryong is on all fours like a beast. Her sister-in-law, alarmed, tries to come between them and save Juryong but is pushed onto the courtyard by the older woman.

"I should chop you into pieces and feed you to the dogs!"

Passersby stop in their tracks and peer through the gate. Some have come from farther away, just to take in the spectacle. Juryong feels no shame, she looks up at the gathering crowd.

Her mother-in-law screams, "Look, everyone! This bitch killed my son. She's a murderer! Throw her in jail!"

Tears blur Juryong's vision at these words. Me, murderer of my own husband? Of all the injustices. When someone once told me I saved his life. Is it my sin that I couldn't save him in the end?

Guilt forces her to lower her head. She couldn't rein in the boy's enthusiasm to go to battle, no doubt it is her fault her husband is dead. Her mother-in-law screams herself hoarse.

"What are you doing down there! Go fetch the police!"

Screamed at, her sister-in-law stops cowering and scurries away through the crowd like she's been doused in hot water. Juryong lets her mother-in-law drag her this way and that by the hair as her consciousness slips. The gaze of the murmuring crowd seems to call for her punishment for a crime she didn't commit.

JAIL

Crowded.

Hot.

She's forgotten the season.

Thirsty.

Despite the stench.

The jail doesn't distinguish men from women, all who are accused are thrown in, like a kind of hell. When one leaves, two enter.

For the first two days or so, she wanted to talk to someone, anyone, but most of the people in there with her are Chinese and don't understand her. There's a woman about Juryong's age who says she's in for stealing barley from a Chinese house. And why was Juryong there? Murder? The woman stops talking to Juryong. It isn't fair, but she is so hungry and exhausted after two days in the cell that she thinks it's better she doesn't have to talk to anyone.

What's going to happen to me now? Be branded a murderer, go to jail? A Chinese jail, where no one understands a word I say?

Hugging her knees to not touch anyone around her, she's lost in thought. Sure, at first she had thought it was indeed her fault that Jeonbin died, but the more she thinks about it, the more unfair it seems that she has to spend years of her life in prison for a crime she didn't commit. A year of married life, half a year in the liberation movement, half a year with her parents—two full years and three calendar years dedicated to her husband, and look what she has to show for it.

But even with such thoughts, she can't find it in her to resent Jeonbin.

There's no light coming from outside, just a light bulb that never goes out. The only mark of time is when the guards change shifts.

On about the fifth day, the barley thief collapses. The people around her complain loudly. They're mostly Chinese and she can't understand what they say, but the Koreans say her inability to sit up makes less room for everyone else. Maybe she is dead. Juryong's heart pounds at the thought. Maybe she is next.

Some are taken out of the jail because their charges are dismissed, and more are taken out like the barley thief. The Chinese can talk to the police and come to some kind of deal, but the Koreans have no recourse. No one takes care of her; she hasn't had a drop of water since her incarceration. When she sweats, she licks the sweat. She tries not to go to the toilet. There are no walls to the toilet, and she has to push through the others to get to the toilet. When she's done, her seat is gone. At first, she refrained because it was uncomfortable, then because it was shameful, but now, she doesn't go to the toilet because she has no reason to.

A few hours after the barley thief was dragged out, about ten Chinese are released at once. The murmurs suggest they'd been accused of being in some movement. There's finally room to stretch a little. Juryong watches the people in the cell help each other and she gets up as well. She staggers before she can stand up straight and falls directly on someone's foot. The Chinese person who had a woman fall on her through no fault of her own shouts something—Juryong assumes they're curses and gets up again. The day isn't over before the cell fills up again.

She is so starved she can vomit, and the world around her seems to sway.

But when she changes her position, her vision comes back to normal.

Only briefly. Soon, her stomach and trachea seem to shrivel into themselves, pulling in the tongue from her mouth. That's how thirsty she feels.

Her tongue is so dry it won't stick to the roof of her mouth. This is death...

Juryong buries her face in her knees. How easily a person's life ends... No effort at all... She's so dizzy that her thoughts don't cohere. She loses track of time.

"Zhang Zhouyong!" shouts a Chinese policeman from the other side of the bars. He calls out several times.

An annoyed Korean turns and says, "Who is Kang Juryong?"

Juryong—who hadn't recognized her name in Chinese—is so startled that she jumps to her feet.

"Me, me! That's me."

The people around her look up and slowly slide over to make way for her. Juryong gingerly makes her way toward the bars, her feet barely given room. The policeman opens the door and talks rapidly to her utter incomprehension. The Korean who had called her name sees her confused expression and translates.

"He's telling you to get out."

"But... charged for the murder..."

"Lack of evidence. No evidence you killed someone."

Dazed, she leaves the police station to find that it's midday. No telling how many nights she was in that cell. The sunlight stabs her eyes.

Alive... I'm alive... I survived that hell.

Juryong closes her eyes. The sunlight shines red through her eyelids as she stands there and gets used to the brilliance. Then, she staggers toward the nearest house she can see. Shamelessly, she begs for food. The woman there is thankfully a Korean who understands her and takes pity on her enough to give her a ball of barley rice.

"Thank you, thank you."

Juryong keeps thanking her as she stuffs the rice into her mouth. She can barely chew it as she has no saliva, and of course her body finds it hard to accept. As soon as she swallows she starts to gag and covers her mouth. The woman who gave her the rice clucks her tongue at her and gets her a gourdful of water to drink. Juryong takes it in with one swallow, spilling much of it down her front.

She walks as slowly as one crawls. The closer she gets to her in-laws' house, the more the ground seems to undulate and swell up toward her, which makes her want to vomit.

From a distance, she looks into the courtyard of her in-laws' house and meets eyes with her sister-in-law. The woman doesn't recognize Juryong at first, but Juryong stares so hard that she finally makes the connection. As Juryong takes a step forward, her sister-in-law shakes her head vigorously. She desperately looks about her, afraid her mother-in-law would appear, and urgently shakes her head again. Juryong can see the fear and exhaustion on her face. This was the end of her relations with her in-laws.

Nothing more did she owe them, or them her.

Pounding her chest to let the undigested barley rice go down, she turns away. They say if one is unlucky enough, one could die of indigestion even from water. But she didn't die, for some reason. Does that make her luckier than those who die from water indigestion? That can't be right.

How easily a person's life ends…

This thought, which she had in jail, keeps looming in her thoughts. It refuses to latch onto anything, but won't go away, either. Her parents' home is fifteen li away.

It is a windy and long road to home.

YELLOW SEA

Her father doesn't have it in him to endure this.

When Juryong was a little girl, she thought her father was worthy of admiration. His lack of affection and general disinterest in his daughter let her down, but there was no doubt that family came first to him. What more could she expect from a father? That's how she felt until she got married.

During the half-year she spent back home, Juryong came to realize she had misunderstood her father for over twenty years. Her father stayed at home not because he cared about his family but because he didn't want to face life in Gando. Even if it was their tenth year since relocation, he still found it a foreign place. That's how hopeless he was. What made it worse was how he dwelled on his past, how he let his pride get the better of him every time. His primary concern was that people would mock him for his daughter who had been thrown out of her husband's home to come back and live with them.

This man, this stupid man... He's no father, he's barely a man.

In the past, Juryong would've chided herself for having such thoughts. But what was she to do now? She couldn't shake the thought that her father was a mediocrity of a man. She'd once had a husband who loved her above his own flesh, and she had held her own with real liberation fighters. They were not all wonderful men, but at the very least they had sharp survival instincts and a readiness for action.

But her father... Well, aside from the fact that he is her father, she really doesn't want much to do with him.

And her thoughts were proven to be true after she came back from jail.

★

"Kang girl!"

Her mother drops the tray she is holding when Juryong stumbles into the courtyard.

"Are you a person or a ghost? Look at the state of you!"

Without hesitation, her mother pulls her into an embrace. Juryong is thankful but also a little annoyed. This isn't the first time she's dragged herself home like this.

Why aren't I crying, did my body run out of water?

These are the thoughts in her head as she hears her mother sob. Then she notices the arms around her are not as thick as they used to be. Just a few days and her mother had lost all that weight. Her mother is turning into a twig.

Juryong waits until her mother pulls herself together before pushing her hoarse voice out her mouth. "Why is the house such a mess?"

The courtyard is piled with their possessions, few that they had.

"Are we about to move?"

Her mother sobs even louder. But it seems like they are, indeed, about to move. And it was probably her father's idea.

"To a different village this time?"

She hadn't held out hope for anyone else, but her mother of course believes in her innocence, that Juryong would never murder her own husband. Or if she had, she had a good reason. Her tears were because of her pity for her daughter who spent a week starving in jail.

Her father is different. Her father's concerns have nothing to do with Juryong's well-being. What her father can't stand is how he's gossip fodder for other people. Whether the allegations are true or not, he doesn't care—his only concern is his pride.

His decision to move away regardless of whether Juryong is found guilty or innocent, or whether she can find them if she gets out, is very much in line with his usual attitude. This is why he never visited her in jail, Juryong suspects. She doesn't feel disappointed because she has always known this is the kind of man he is. It is pointless to resent him for not being otherwise.

"How far is it you want to go that you won't even say it? We're leaving Tonghwahyeon, even?"

She knows her question is futile. She's only trying to get her mother to stop crying.

"Korea..." Her mother barely gets the word out of her mouth. "Korea, your father wants to go back."

If they'd tried to move within Gando, then Juryong could've tracked them down eventually if she'd found them gone—but Korea? They really tried to get rid of her.

"I shouldn't have come back."

"How could you say that? All I did was wait for you."

"Don't worry about me."

She's not merely saying that to reassure her mother. It really was all right. She would've felt disappointment had she not known what kind of man her father is. But she knows.

Her father comes home around sunset and says nothing to Juryong when he sees her. He's not thrilled the daughter who ruined their reputations is back, but she's a useful worker and they're about to leave Manchuria, which means it'll be more gain than loss if she stayed. Juryong doesn't pretend to be glad to see him either.

★

Even as she helps pack, or lays down straw in the rabbit hutch with the rabbits they will all harvest soon, or spoons her rice into her mouth at the tray table, or wakes up out of breath from a nightmare, she has the same thought.

I didn't kill him. I didn't kill him.

But sometimes, she's confused.

Did I kill him?

Did I leave him there to die?

How wonderful it would've been if she'd had another place to go to besides home. She's also worried about the others. How is Oga? And the men who helped her bury Jeonbin? And General Baek?

There is no way to talk to any of them now. This isn't any different from when she was fourteen and had to flee Pyongyang with her parents. The house they lived in now belongs to someone else, and so does their land. Could any of her friends remember her?

Only the grave she buried her husband in remains the same.

Juryong can't let go of thoughts of Jeonbin. The only evidence that she ever lived in Gando, now buried elsewhere.

★

Ten days by road, crossing the Amlok River, then a train at Sinu-iju. The path they took around ten years ago. Her brother had been little enough to be carried by her mother back then, but now he complains of how much he has to walk. The adults are too tired to humor his crankiness.

After a whole day on the train, they get off at Sariwon past Pyongyang. Juryong wonders why Sariwon instead of Ganggye or Pyongyang. But it makes no difference to her in the end, whether she understands the reason or not. She's just an empty vessel, tethered to her father.

They have no connections there but manage to find a place to live without difficulty. Their landlord will waive their rent as long as they help with the farming and some heavy work, and even give them a patch for their own vegetables in the spring. Harvest season is upon them, which means it's too late to find sharecropper work, so this is ideal. If they take in some needlework and other tasks here and there, the four of them just might survive. Juryong's brother is soon going to be old enough to work as well. It's a relief, the thought of work and an honest life.

After cleaning up their new home and finishing their unpacking, Juryong falls into a dreamless, deep sleep for the first time in a long while.

★

As soon as the sun is up, Juryong takes her father to their landlord's. They are to show up that morning to see what work needs to be done. On the first day, they weed the sesame field and tie heads of cabbage with string. None of the work requires much skill, but Juryong is naturally deft with her hands, which elicits praise from the other workers.

The landlord is a generationally wealthy farmer who has come down a bit in the world but still has considerable property. The women who work with Juryong tell her this.

These women are also tenants who borrow land to farm. Each sharecropper takes turns sending someone to the landlord's house to help with the work there. The women are all about Juryong's mother's age.

Her father, dragged out here by Juryong, mostly blinks inanely as he pretends to work, and around lunchtime he's called out by the landlord. Juryong tries to be generous and looks at it from his point of view. She supposes he's embarrassed by having to work with so many women. Maybe he's trying to be a better father than before and finds it harder than he thought.

Juryong arrives home as the sun is about to set. Her mother greets her, tired from household work, caring for her brother, and the extra needlework she's taken in besides.

"Where's Father?" they ask each other at the same time.

Her mother asks what she did with her father whom she took with her this morning, and Juryong wonders aloud where he's gone when he had left work early. Her mother hesitates as to whether to start dinner without him and decides to feed only the little one when he cries for his dinner. Just as she's putting away those dishes, Juryong's father arrives.

"You're home!" Where could he have been, in this place where they knew not a single person yet? Juryong's mother takes a step forward to greet him then averts her face.

"Your breath stinks of drink!"

"What money do you have for drinks?" interjects Juryong, her voice sharp. Her father, drunk, talks more than he normally does. Already bad at talk, alcohol makes it worse. But it seems he was called forth by the landlord in a welcome drink, and her father had intended to have only one drink but it turned out a friend of her father's was in-laws with the landlord and so they were practically family and it would be rude to just get up after a drink and they were around the same age after all—

"But you're not family! And did this friend of yours lift a finger for you when we fled from Pyongyang?"

Her mother grabs Juryong's shoulder and holds her back.

"You silly girl, I can get a drink if I want to, what's it to you?" Her father scoffs and goes into his room. Juryong breathes deeply, wondering if she went too far this time. Her father is no lush, no reason to get angry over a tipsy afternoon. Maybe befriending the landlord is a good idea, even.

But what of her mother who had delayed her dinner in wait for him? Juryong had a good lunch with the other women at the landlord's house, but her mother, who had taken care of her brother all day and cared for the house and even taken in needlework?

She cannot summon any guilt toward her father. Juryong hesitates for a long time in the courtyard to give it a chance but gives up to go back to her room.

★

As cold as Korea can get, it's nothing compared to Manchuria. That first winter in Sariwon, none of Juryong's family catches the flu, which has never happened before.

Every three days, Juryong goes to the landlord's house. Even in winter there is much work to be done. There is hay to be twisted into rope, herbs to be dried, firewood to procure, laundry to do by smashing the ice in the river, and buckets to fill. The pay affords them food and the leftover rope can be woven into shoes.

On days she's home, Juryong helps with the housework and the needlework. It's not a lot of money, but perhaps, if they're frugal enough, they can afford a bit of land of their own. A dream that swells her heart.

Her father is a step removed from all this. Men will be men, but his drinks with the landlord become more and more frequent.

Juryong used to chide him about his responsibilities as a father to feed his family that he dragged out to a faraway place, but soon she tires of this and ignores him instead. Better to make one more stitch or fill one more bucket of water than waste that time in argument with her father.

The landlord at least seems to be a better man than her father. He doesn't seem to have ever carried resentment for another in his heart. They do say riches beget generosity. Never having experienced a day of hardship in his life, he can afford to be kind and charitable. Since this can only be gained through luck and not talent or hard work, it is a way of life completely beyond Juryong, but as the man gives them their wages in a timely manner and doesn't give them cause for grief, there is no reason to think badly of him.

One time, the landlord takes Juryong's side when her father yells at her as she works in the landlord's courtyard.

"That girl is so headstrong, what man would ever take her? She's my own flesh and blood but she scares me with her harshness."

"She's a good and clever worker, you're worrying about nothing. I wish she were in my family."

Juryong sweeps the snow in the courtyard even harder. How could that near stranger of a man understand her better than her own father? Tears well at the thought. Jeonbin was raised in a gentle manner as well, maybe in time he would've become a man like the landlord if he'd had time.

Jeonbin...

She shakes her head and thinks of something else.

I wish that man was our father instead.

No. That is too much to ask. She is fine with the landlord not being her father. She just wishes her father wasn't her father, either.

Winter passes into fall. Juryong's family, as promised, is granted tenancy on two rice paddies and a vegetable patch.

There's a solid kind of joy in how some handiwork at home turns into money, but even that joy pales in the face of growing one's own food.

And they'd been granted more land than expected. This year, her little brother was to help out. Their lazy father was useless, and they would need more hands if they wanted to farm all that land and help out at the landlord's house as well.

"How could you send this little baby out into the fields?"

Her mother tries to stop her from shaking awake her brother at dawn to teach him to carry water for the paddies. Her brother whines, still half-asleep, and ends up in tears.

"A ten-year-old crying such big tears!" scolds Juryong. Her brother clings to her mother's chest and her father turns his back on them, clearing his throat distastefully.

"Babies a head shorter than Dongie go out into the fields to work. How long are you going to let him cling to you and not pull his weight around here?"

"Maybe the rice paddies can come later and we teach him the vegetable patch instead, all right? That seems right."

Well, it was true he would probably spend his whole time in a tantrum if she took him to the rice paddy now. But even so, shouldn't they get him ready to work? Isn't it better to prepare him instead of coddle him? What if he grew up to become as useless as her father?

These words come up to her throat but turn into a sigh instead.

"Fine. Do what you want."

Both the rice paddies and vegetable patch become the sole work of Juryong and her mother. And her mother is needed in the house so much, there are more days when Juryong leaves the house without her.

And she still works some days at the landlord's house. She wishes her brother or father would take care of that obligation at least, but the landlord insists on "Kang girl" to come, as she's so good at work.

She tills and plants there as well, but it can't be as fun as the same work on her own fields. She gets into the habit of running back there after her duties at the landlord's. That means working from dawn to dusk. Only when she's worked on her own fields around sundown does she feel like she can lie down that night. She's determined to put in as much blood and sweat into her own fields as the landlord's.

The summer is hot but there's no drought, we can expect a good harvest.

The thought is enough to erase her fatigue. Every day as she walks from the landlord's to her home, she calculates how much they'd have left of their crop after their tithe to the landlord. No matter how many times she calculates it, she never gets tired of it.

The spring and summer pass like a dream. The days get shorter, and the body feels heavier and slower. Once the harvest is over and Chuseok passes, we'll buy bolts of cotton and make new clothes and new winter blankets filled with cotton wool... The very thought speeds up her hands and feet.

She comes home one day and finds that even her father is home early. As she's about to enter the kitchen with some snails she's picked up on her way to suggest boiling in a stew, her father nonchalantly says to her, "Kang girl, get ready to marry."

Juryong dumps her pile of snails into her mother's apron so fast that a few of the shells crack. She stomps out of the kitchen.

"Get ready for *what*?"

"You're getting married."

"Why are you talking this nonsense?"

Her father shakes his head and gets up from the porch to go to his room. Her mother, when the coast is clear, comes out of the kitchen to speak to her.

"You better do as your father says. How thankful you should be! He heard about your banishment in Gando but decided to marry you anyway."

"What banishment? When did Jeonbin ever banish me?"

Her mother grips her trembling shoulders. This doesn't calm her. The older woman's hands are cold, and they sap the heat from Juryong's blood.

"Fine," says Juryong. "Say I get married. Who takes care of the family? You'll do everything on our own?

"Why are you the one to worry about that?"

Juryong shouts, "Is there anyone else worrying about it?"

Her father slides open his door and peeks out. "You fool! Worry about yourself. Whoever heard of a young widow living the rest of her life with her parents?"

His words are almost impressively sharp for her slow and silent father. The sight of her father, so preoccupied with propriety, raising his voice at her is enough to strike her speechless. He doesn't stop there.

"We allow this broken girl into our home and the ingrate attacks us? Even beasts have more decency."

Juryong thinks of the snails she brought. The ones that desperately crawl over each other in search of a way out. How many had she stepped on just now? Barely alive but about to turn into putrid, dead messes. That's what "broken" means.

But tears mean defeat. She bites down on her tongue, which makes the tears recede.

"Fine. Tell me about this man you want to throw me away to."

Her mother, still gripping her shoulders, forces a smile and says in a pleasant voice, "You know the landlord thinks highly of you?"

The wife he had when young had died before giving him a child. Juryong understands their intentions, but it still leaves her flabbergasted.

"You, you want me to marry a man old enough to be my uncle? Me?"

Repulsive. So the reason the landlord had been kind to her was not because of his own goodness but because he had seen her as a potential wife? She wants to jump up and down in fury.

Rumors must've spread because the other women who help out at the man's house subtly avoid her. The complaints of why a man who lives alone has so much laundry or his silliness at having a fire at even the hottest times of the year because of his bad knees and back disappear before her. Juryong is their future landlady, as far as they're concerned. They better be careful, they seem to think.

The landlord wants her to move in after the harvest. The absence of a ceremony, as much as she doesn't want this marriage, makes her think she's some bit of property being acquired and moved from one place to another. Something that can be replaced when worn out, something to pass on from house to house and pay a day wage for a job well done. Juryong's family is promised a bit of land and their house to own. As payment for Juryong herself.

The landlord summons her to the house more often. He wants her to get used to how the house is managed. The most he does is ask her to wipe down the floors, but knowing what the old man wants, even that bit of work disgusts her. The man is on the neat side, but from time to time, a thing that disgusts her more is caught in the rag she uses to wipe the floors. The old man's wavy, slightly faded, pubic hair.

"Juryong, come in here."

He's calling for her. Juryong, who is laying out chili peppers to dry on the porch, doesn't bother to look up at him as she dusts her hands on her apron and gets up.

"Leave that and go home now. Give your father these papers."

Inside the landlord's room are some papers where the ink hasn't even dried yet. Juryong stands there awkwardly as the old man leaves the room, as if to give her time. She looks down at the papers. They're a mix of Hangul and Hanja and she can't read all of it, but the gist is clear enough. She is to be betrothed to him in return for ownership of the house and the land they are tenants of.

He wanted me to see this, that's why he left me with them. That this is how much he pays for me, so I better be worth it.

That a piece of paper should hold so much power.

She moves it aside and positions a fresh new sheet. If a piece of paper can decide her fate, she can play at this as well. She picks up the slender brush the landlord had put down. Her hand trembles. She gathers her right sleeve with her left hand away from the paper and writes a line.

Mother, read this.

But does her mother even know how to read? She's never thought about this before. After a moment's hesitation, she dips the brush into the inkstone and thinks that if her mother can't read this, her father will. She's mentioned her mother, but her father will know that the words are really meant for him.

Think of me as dead to you.

Her handwriting is so bad it almost doesn't matter if her mother or father know how to read. Jeonbin had persisted in teaching her how to write despite how ugly she wrote—quickly, she shakes her head and pulls herself together. No telling when the landlord would be back.

She blows on the wet letters, folds the note, and slips it into her tunic before doing as the landlord told, folding his letter and walking out of the room with it in her hand, a nonchalant expression on her face. She ignores the women coming back to the landlord's house from the fields, who see her come out of the landlord's room and start to whisper.

Juryong will leave. Instead of the landlord's letter she will leave her own and walk out of there as if headed for dawn work but go far, farther than the landlord's house. She will tear up the landlord's letter and scatter them on her way. She will go where no one knows her and she knows no one. Nothing and nobody will steal her heart.

She covers the ink stain on her tunic with one hand as she makes her way home.

PART II

PYONGYANG

1

"If you find any pictures of those bob-haired modern girls, give them to Juryong!"

The words reach Juryong's ears over the relentless clatter of the factory machines. She peers around at the direction of the voice.

"Did you all hear me? Juryong collects pictures of the modern girls."

I knew it, that older Hong woman, the busiest of busybodies in all of Pyongyang.

All the same, Juryong likes her. She raises a hand and plays along. "She's right! Pictures of modern girls! Bring them all to me."

"What do you even do with them? What a strange thing to collect, they're not even movie stars."

Juryong glances in the direction of this other voice as she brings her hand back to her work. She has no time to waste like this if she wants to make her allotted quota for the day.

"What," says the woman Hong, "does this mean you yourself collect photos of handsome movie stars?"

"But weren't you the one who gave them to me, hyungnim? Who here is falling for your feigned innocence?"

The other factory girls continue in this vein, their giggles mixing in with the smell of the spinning petroleum rollers. This rare moment of lightness is soon doused out by the foreman.

"Shut your traps, you need your mouths to work?"

They clam up at his words. The room is soon filled again with the sound of machines turning and the smell of heated rubber.

The foreman overseeing the shoemaking section, where Juryong works, is notorious for beating workers like animals. And not only with his hands. Anything he grabs turns into a weapon.

Hands and broom handles are one thing, at least they are somewhat ritualistically proper implements of violence against a fellow human being. But half-baked rubber shoes and petroleum-soaked rollers? Never mind the physical pain, it's the fact that they're not even seen as people that cuts them to the bone.

When the foreman is in a good mood he ignores their chatter, but when he's not, even the sound of clearing one's throat can send him flying into a rage. The slightest excuse is enough to start him pounding on his unfortunate victim.

And he has a rule where each new factory worker has to be taught this by example.

Four months ago, on Juryong's first day, it was Hong's turn. Even Juryong, who had seen some violence in her day, was so terrified at how frenzied the beating had been and how little Hong had resisted, that she was frozen on the spot. When she came to her senses and tried to go to Hong and help her up, the other factory women held her back, whispering that if she did that, the foreman would only beat Hong again until she was off her feet once more. Only when the foreman strode out of the room huffing and puffing did Hong get up on her own and dust herself off. The next morning, Hong walked with a limp from having had her ankle stamped on.

"I'm fine, young lady. He just wanted to make an example of me for the new girl."

"An example?"

"When there's a new girl, he just grabs whoever he wants and beats her like you just saw. Showing you what he can do to you if you cross him."

"But aren't words enough? Who treats another person like that?"

"Don't think of yourself as a person. Then you'll be fine."

Of course, the foreman does more than beat people.

Juryong's section assembles rubber cutouts into shoes. No matter how quick they are with their hands and skilled at the work, it's almost impossible to complete forty pairs of shoes in a day. On her first day, Juryong, aside from the ones that had to be binned, completed only five pairs. Learning how to make them took half a day, and she had painstakingly managed to complete seven before her shift was over, two of them being so shoddy she wouldn't even give them to a beggar. Forget the quota, she thought. She hoped she wouldn't be fired on her first day.

She glumly stood by her pile awaiting inspection when the foreman grabbed a few good pairs from the other workers' piles next to her and tossed them onto hers.

"What's the meaning of this?"

Juryong wasn't trying to start an argument, she was only surprised and wanted to know what was going on, but the way her words came out ended up surprising her even more. The foreman gave her a once-over, scoffed, and tossed the other workers' shoes back to their original piles.

"Everyone, go home."

Juryong had closed her eyes. The foreman was only being considerate, she thought. Of course I wouldn't do well on my first day and he wanted to raise the average a bit! I hope the other workers don't think I'm a proud fool for declining his favor.

But as soon as the foreman left, the other workers immediately crowded around Juryong's workstation and patted her back.

"You did well!"

"Good for you!"

What had she done well? She was bewildered as the other workers hugged her shoulders and smiled at her.

The next day she completed ten pairs, the day after that, thirteen. Her numbers went up little by little, but until she hit twenty-five pairs, she was hit on the head at the end of each day. Why was that necessary when she was already taking a pay cut for not making quota? Wasn't that punishment enough? More than the pain, it was the rage and sorrow that brought tears to her eyes.

Only a long while later did a worker tell her that the foreman had been trying to spoil the camaraderie on the factory floor with his fake generosity. That he always did so for teams that looked particularly close-knit. That Juryong showed from the very beginning such fakeness wouldn't work with her, and he was punishing her for it.

"Let none of us quit so he would never have to replace any of us."

Juryong nodded, agreeing to this collective resolve.

I can't stop anyone from quitting, but at the very least, I can stay. If I quit, someone new will be hired and another person will be made an example of. At the very least, I can prevent someone from getting beaten on my account.

★

She hadn't intended to come back to Pyongyang. Nor had she imagined she'd become a worker at a rubber factory.

All the money she had scraped together barely amounted to a train ticket to even the nearest stop. If she didn't leave Sariwon quickly, she'd only get caught that much faster. She ended up jumping on the train without a ticket. And the station where she had disembarked in her attempt to avoid the ticket collector just happened to be near Pyongyang. Had it only been ten years since she'd been there last?

Its streets were now strewn with stars. She'd known since she was a child that Pyongyang was one of the great cities of Korea but after the mountains of Gando and the farm in Sariwon, Pyongyang rips her horizons wide open. The gisaeng women in their flashy clothes walking down the paved streets, the modern boys in their fedoras and three-piece suits. Such sights stirred her heart, but the future also weighed heavily...

Oh brother, I'm still young, I can take care of myself, what's there to possibly worry about?

In a discarded newspaper, she looked up places where she could stay or work. She secured a rented room with a lie about having found employment, and in the application for a factory job, she matter-of-factly wrote down the address she had not even slept in yet. She couldn't help but congratulate herself on her own cleverness.

For the first few months, she did think about how long she'd have to work before going back to Gando. She would have to go back, her husband's grave was there, not to mention her old comrades. But life in Pyongyang was full of unexpected joys. The work was hard, but there's pleasure in earning and spending her own money, pleasure in the company of peers. Before this, she had spent her whole adult life in small villages where she didn't have much chance to befriend women her age.

Those who were standoffish and territorial when she said she was from Gando would immediately change their tune when she added she was born in Ganggye and lived as a child in Pyongyang—they treated her like a childhood friend. And thus, with no real reason to leave Pyongyang or go to Gando, Juryong decided to stay where she was for the time being.

★

Sitting around a large pot of cooking barley that smells faintly of processed rubber, the workers mix in the banchan they each brought from home and make a bibimbap to share. Every lunch is like this. The rubber factory job had caught her interest because it had advertised that lunch was free, but what they had meant was that the barley was free, and everyone was required to bring their own banchan. There are some who hate the smell of rubber so much they bring their own rice, but for most of them, with all the salty banchan mixed in, the taste isn't too far from tolerable.

Samnyuh, hired a little after Juryong, brightly asks her a question with her eyes wide.

"So what do you plan on doing after work today?"

Samnyuh ranks the lowest in terms of seniority, but she's the same age as Juryong, which means only two others in their section are older. Samnyuh shares a surname with one of these older women, Hong, prompting them to delightedly wonder out loud if they're related. It's bad enough parents are so careless with naming daughters—Samnyuh meaning "third daughter"—but with her surname being Hong, Hong Samnyuh has been destined since birth to be nicknamed "Hongsam" or "Ginseng" for the rest of her life. But she is a friendly and generous soul, who only smiles when even the younger factory girls tease her by calling her "Ginseng, hey Ginseng."

"Well, I thought I'd go to the cinema and then maybe take a walk."

"What's the cinema like, is the price worth it?"

Since even the third-tier seats cost a day's wage for a factory girl, the cinema is indeed an expensive proposition. Juryong herself has gone for her first and only time last month. She dozed off in the middle of it, tired as she was from work, but the simple fact of having gone to the cinema for the first time in her life was enough to make her feel proud. Already she has plans to buy hardboiled eggs and drinks like everyone else the next time, and to never, ever fall asleep.

"My," Hong shouts, "since our 'Ryong doesn't need to cook for her dead husband, she's the real lucky one!"

Everyone falls into an appalled silence. The sudden tension in the air startles Hong into realizing her carelessness.

Juryong jokes, "You don't need to remind us, everyone knows how lucky I am!"

The spell is broken and the other workers grin, both reassured and reassuring.

Still, I've got to be careful with how I talk about my hobbies, no need to flaunt my freedom, even if it comes at a cost.

She smiles back at the factory girls sitting across from her and takes a last spoonful of the barley mixed into greens. A bell goes off, signaling the end of lunch.

Juryong doesn't want to marry again, and without a family to worry over, has no interest in acquiring houses or land, either. Acquiring a taste for coffee is more her speed now. All she cares about is enjoying herself in her own modest way. Going to the cinema. Getting a dress made. Trying on shiny shoes and those modern silk stockings.

If I don't spend on myself this money I made by eating rubber-flavored barley, who do I spend it on?

But dresses and shiny shoes are out of the question on a factory girl's pay. Those frivolous bits of clothing cost more than a month's rent. All she has left of a month's pay after rent, food, and other essentials is about five or six won. She would save two or three won of that and dare spend the rest on trying to be one of the modern girls.

Sitting in a café in her non-Western garb gets her ignored by the waitresses, or sometimes worse—their hostile attention. Her order evaporates as the waitresses deliver the coffee of people who arrive later than she does and bring her drink out only after a long delay. She wonders how much money they make. Should she have become a waitress instead? She is never going to get a modern dress made at this rate, but maybe she could at least cut her hair short. If she gets a bob first, maybe she would look like she's at least trying to fit in with the modern girls, despite her clothes.

These preoccupations hold her over until the end of work.

Her rented room depresses her. It makes her think of the husband she hasn't held in over a year. Of her family trying to sell her off for a house and fields. At least she feels less lonely when her landlady's daughter comes to share her bed, but this daughter also just got a job at a factory and is coming home late, pushing Juryong deeper into her modern-girl fantasies.

Let's forget about the cinema today and go for a walk instead.

The days are getting longer, and it's still bright after work. Juryong wanders the streets of downtown Pyongyang until the sun sets, musing at all the things she can and cannot buy with her money, and after much deliberation, purchases a magazine doing a special feature on the New Woman.

★

"'Ryong! 'Ryong!"

It's Ginseng. Juryong tries to ignore her because the foreman could be watching. Ginseng grabs her by the sleeve.

"Hey Juryong, look over here for a minute."

"Catch your breath first! What's going on?"

"I brought this for you."

Ginseng hands her some pictures of a modern girl: pencil sketches on blank pages torn from a magazine and a sheet of scratch paper. The sketched woman is slim and tall wearing a tweed skirt and jacket, a glamorous beauty. Her hair is of course cut short underneath a hat with a narrow brim. What makes Juryong smile is the arrow on the left pointing to her with "Ryong" written in the same pencil.

"Hey Ginseng," Juryong says, speaking in a low voice so the foreman won't catch them.

"What?"

"You drew this?"

Ginseng, excitement in her eyes, nods, eager to hear what Juryong thinks.

"Are you blind, my friend? I'm nothing like her!" Her words come out hurtful, not at all what she intended, and Ginseng's face falls.

"I mean," says Juryong quickly, "they're beautiful drawings. I had no idea you had such talent."

Ginseng begins to lighten up.

"They're not really my drawings, I just have these others that I really like, I copied them by hand because I wanted to share them with you."

"Oh, I see, then of course I don't look like them. But what skill you have! I don't even think of copying any drawing I like. My hand doesn't listen to my mind."

A blush spreads on Ginseng's face, but she doesn't seem to mind Juryong's words. Juryong puts the palm-sized drawings together and decadently waves them like a fan.

"Anyway, thanks so much. After our friend Hong made fun of me the other day, you're the only one who thought to comfort me with drawings of real modern girls."

Hearing her name, Hong bursts in on their conversation. "Is someone talking about me?"

Juryong hands her the drawings, which Hong swiftly whips through. Her eyes grow wide.

"Ginseng drew these?"

The two other women nod, which makes Hong fuss and pass on the pictures as she begs Ginseng to make her some sketches, too. Now that Hong knows of Ginseng's talent, their entire section would soon know as well. Juryong smiles, pleased. Hong's fussing draws interest from the other women, who stretch their hands, also wanting to take a look. While the foreman is away, Ginseng's modern girls flaunt their chicness at each workstation.

"Hey, careful with those, don't smudge them."

They ignore Juryong's plea, too busy examining Ginseng's handiwork, reaching for them and passing them among themselves. As the pictures make their way back across the room, Juryong cranes her neck to check their progress. It would be terrible if the foreman walked in right now.

"What's all this ruckus?"

The foreman suddenly appears right behind Juryong. Her heart leaps to her throat, but she tries to calm herself thinking, It's all right, it's all right. As long as we don't get caught with the pictures. And what is this worthless man going to do if he caught us, anyway? The pictures have already arrived at the next workstation. She can just about get them back if she stretches her hand and then stuff them into her inner tunic. But this damn foreman refuses to move from behind her. As Juryong bends the rubber into the requisite shape, she feels a flow of sweat as wide as the Daedong River run down her back.

"Show me what you have in your fist. What is this interesting thing that you're keeping from me?"

They are caught. Dread fills Juryong's vision with darkness, and she sighs. The factory girl next to her who had tried to hide the pictures in her hand darts her gaze toward Juryong, then to the foreman and bows repeatedly.

"I am sorry, sir, so sorry, sir."

"Did I say anything? I just wanted to share the fun. It's you girls making me out to be bad."

"It is our fault."

"Shut up. Hand over what you've got there."

The foreman forces open the trembling factory girl's fingers and snatches away the pictures. Everyone pretends not to look as they're bent over their workstations, but they try to glimpse what the foreman is doing. The foreman calmly shuffles through the pictures and cackles at the last one.

"Kang Juryong as a modern girl?"

Juryong being the only worker in her section with the syllable "ryong" in her name, she is immediately identified. As an unfamiliar shame spreads, Juryong closes her eyes. The strength leaves her hands and she can't even pretend to work anymore.

"Kang Juryong, tell me. So you're really a modern girl? Have I been overlooking this genuine modern girl in our midst all this time? I haven't been treating you properly, then."

Mocking, he goes to stand in front of Juryong. The sight of him crumpling each picture one by one makes Juryong bite her lip. She can almost hear the heat expel from her breath. Suddenly, the foreman kicks out Juryong's stool from under her and she sprawls to the floor. Is this really something she deserves a beating for? But then again, reason was never something that stopped the foreman from beating a worker.

It just happens to be my turn today; I have to bear it. I swear I won't cry out no matter how hard he kicks me.

Against expectations, the foreman doesn't kick her. Juryong has her head wrapped in her arms, her body relaxed and ready for the blows. When she glances up to see what's taking him so long, he grabs her by the hair.

"Hey, don't modern girls have short hair? Look here, someone bring me the scissors."

The words break Juryong's resolve, and she begins to scream.

Entertained, the foreman shakes her head by his fistful of her hair.

Petrified as they are, no one dares to move as the foreman repeatedly demands for shears. He shakes her head a few times more and jerks it back so her ear is near his mouth, as if he wants to whisper to her. But what he says is loud enough for all the factory girls to hear.

"If Kang Juryong is a modern girl, she and I should get some free love."

Juryong's face turns crimson with fury. She wants to cuss him out but the fear of retribution toward her fellow workers stops the words in her throat.

"Wouldn't you like that? You enjoy free love, right? Aren't you a modern girl?"

Someone begins to sob. Juryong can't see above the line of workstations. Who's crying? I can hear her blocking her mouth and trying to hold it in. Who's crying for me? The thought brings tears to Juryong's own eyes.

"What have you got to cry about, huh?"

The foreman slaps Juryong on the forehead and slaps her cheeks as well between every word. As if that wasn't enough, he slams her head against the floor before letting go of her and dusting his hands. With difficulty, he gets up from his crouching position, swaying a bit and panting. The factory women who had been sneaking looks in silence quickly bow their heads and pretend to work.

The foreman clucks his tongue and says loudly, "Modern girls are either students or gisaeng whores."

His words shock the workers' hands into stillness.

"Do you think you're students?"

Silence. The foreman scoffs.

"You're only setting yourselves up as whores if you pretend to be modern girls. Get your head out of the clouds and do some work, you lazy bitches. And if anyone wants to be a modern girl, come to me. I'll make you into a modern girl."

Only when the foreman has left does Juryong uncurl her back and stand on her feet. She flattens out the crumpled pictures and slips them into her tunic. Ginseng must be the one crying; her guess is confirmed when she gets up. Waving away the people rushing toward her to help her, Juryong sits down again at her workstation. Her physical pain will go away, and she can borrow an iron from her landlady to straighten out the pictures. As for poisonous words from an evil man, all she had to do was forget them.

Just because someone says I'm not a modern girl doesn't mean it's true.

The fact that she isn't a modern girl, and her hopes of becoming one looked ridiculous to others—Juryong isn't unaware of it. She thinks of it too much herself to be unaware of it.

But her insecurity isn't because of the foreman. Because really, the foreman can't do a single thing to get in the way of her becoming a modern girl.

And now that she's been castigated by a man of the old world, this means she passed the first rite of passage of a modern girl, if anything.

Juryong concentrates on this fact for the rest of her workday, but when she arrives home, she collapses into tears.

2

"When we lived in Gando, we kept rabbits. You'll never see an animal as clever as a rabbit."

"I love rabbits, I wish we had them, too."

Okkie turns to Juryong and keeps egging her on for more stories. In Okkie's house, where Juryong rents a room, they raise a dog in the yard. A short-tailed, big, yellow dog, ostensibly for keeping watch over the house, but the animal is so gentle it hardly barks at even strangers. An eager friendliness shared by Okkie herself.

"But they multiply into so many little rabbits, and taking care of them is a chore. And the droppings! They eat their own droppings, like dogs."

"Really? Their own droppings?"

"Yes! And not all their droppings, just the ones that still have some meal in them. They sniff them up, like this."

Juryong wriggles her nose like a rabbit would. Okkie bursts into giggles.

"And?"

"And what?"

"And what else do rabbits do?"

"Hmm, what else. Oh, I know!"

"Know what?"

"Rabbits can die of loneliness."

"You're lying."

"Really."

"You're lying!"

"Really!"

"A rabbit dying of loneliness? It's not even human!"

Juryong scoffs. "And a human dying of loneliness makes sense?"

Okkie thinks about this for a moment before shaking her head. "It's the same with humans when we say someone dies of loneliness. We're just saying that, you know? If someone has actually ever died of loneliness, I'd like to hear about it."

Juryong is about to answer but decides not to. Of course Okkie has never known loneliness. This is a child who is so sick of sleeping in the same room as her younger siblings and parents that she comes over to the renter's room to sleep—deathly loneliness is probably something she actually craves.

After tossing and turning a bit, Okkie makes a declaration into the darkness.

"I want to grow up quickly and live alone like Juryong hyungnim."

"What do you mean, alone? I'm living with Okkie now."

"Oh hyungnim. You know what I mean, stop joking!"

"Go to sleep. You'll be late for the factory tomorrow."

"I don't want to go."

"You have to be diligent if you want to be a real adult, no?"

"My legs are so itchy I can't go to sleep."

Okkie kicks her blanket a few times and groans. Still a child, that one. Juryong remembers being that young and how her limbs also itched from unspent strength. Ever since getting that job at the silk factory, Okkie was finding it hard to fall asleep at night.

Well, that's what happens when you're made to sit in one place all day, doing something you're not used to doing. It's irritating to hear the young woman whipping her limbs through the sheets, but she lets her vent. Here was this girl, younger than the brother Juryong had left behind in Sariwon, making a living at a factory. At home, they treat Okkie like an adult. Which means she has no one to complain to except Juryong.

The thought makes her gently pat Okkie's belly, calming her twisting and turning. "If it helps you get sleepy, I'll tell you more about Gando."

"Finally. What took you so long to get the hint? Go right ahead."

"How about you sing me a song, and I'll tell you a story?"

"Hyungnim should go first."

"You want me to sing?"

"No, silly, tell me the story."

★

General Baek Gwangwoon died the year Juryong left Gando. She learned this on the train coming from Sariwon to Pyongyang as she eavesdropped on the two men across from her. They'd slipped her suspicious looks—but what harm could come of a girl in such shabby clothes? How could they have possibly imagined that the grubby little woman in front of them had once fought under the command of General Baek and even ridden a train with him? Juryong felt the breath knocked out of her body as if a very large and cold hand had wrapped itself around her. She tried hard to fix her features, not that her feelings would've registered with the men.

In Pyongyang, she searched far and wide for rumors about General Baek's demise as she asked around and looked for old newspapers. It was that June when the Tongeuibu collapsed due to infighting and joined the Korean Provisional Government in

Shanghai and changed its name to Chameuibu. Three months later, their old Tongeuibu comrade Moon Hakbin ambushed them in an attack. Meanwhile, she'd spent the last year thinking that General Baek must still be fighting the good fight on the battlefield...

Though Juryong thought herself an ordinary woman who knew little of the wide world, she had been sure upon first glance that General Baek was a great man. Juryong herself had considered him a comrade from those years when there was no one for her to rely on, how she had put her trust in him like she would in an older brother. How heartbroken her old comrades must be to lose him!

Comrades only because we fought for the same objectives— he still was the greater man for having believed more than I had. My convictions were just a thimbleful's worth compared to his.

How strange to think he died while she survived only for having run away from Gando. How many of the people from her past are left to remember her now? The sorrow crushes her heart.

★

"That Gwangwoon man, was he handsome?"

"Well, you can't beat my Jeonbin for handsome."

"Why bother talking about some man who isn't even handsome?"

"To hear you speak, sometimes."

Annoyed by this drowsy response from Okkie at the end of her story, Juryong turns her back on her, stealing half the blanket.

"It's cold. Give me the blanket."

"Cold? It's summer. Just cover your belly."

"Summer? Isn't it Chuseok in a few days?"

"You always must have the last word."

Despite the annoyance in these last words, Juryong spreads the blanket evenly around them again and tucks Okkie in up to the shoulders. And as Okkie drifts into sleep, the weight of drowsiness falls on her own eyelids.

Feeling like she's barely slept a wink, Juryong shakes Okkie awake the next morning, and the two go and fetch well water to prepare breakfast before leaving for work. Since the silk factory Okkie works at is near Juryong's workplace, she usually walks Okkie there. Juryong looks forward to this so much that she sleeps a little less each night to make the walk with her.

"Be safe at work," says Juryong.

"You too, hyungnim."

Okkie runs to join the other girls from her factory. No longer is it strange to see factory girls who are as young as fourteen, silk spinners like Okkie herself.

The silk factories prefer young unmarried girls while the rubber factory tends to hire older women, some with families of their own. The silk factories have dormitories, which makes hiring women with families difficult. The rubber factories don't always have work and tended to attract workers who needed supplementary income. Okkie was an exceptional case who didn't have to live in the dorms because she could commute from home, and even then, they had to call in a personal favor to make this arrangement possible.

If there was no overtime, the two walked home together. It was rare that the rubber factory would have overtime, which often meant it was Juryong who needed to wait for Okkie at the gates of the silk factory. If girls Okkie's age were coming out, that meant work was over, and if no one came out, that meant overtime. Now that the days were longer, even if there were no girls coming out of the factory, Juryong would wait until sunset.

Okkie emerges from the silk factory completely steamed from the cooking silkworm cocoons. Working at a rubber factory isn't easy either, but the sight of Okkie makes Juryong feel so sorry for the girl that she walks up to her and immediately fans Okkie's face.

"Good job today."

"You too, hyungnim."

On the way home, Juryong hears Okkie humming a song she hasn't heard before.

"What's that song? How sad the melody is."

"Something the other girls taught me during lunch."

"Sing it for me."

O life running through this desolate plain
Where are you going
In this lonely world full of harsh suffering
What are you looking for so desperately

"Okkie, do you understand that song?"

"What else can it mean besides what it says?"

Okkie continues to sing the song in her still-childlike voice. Juryong would normally praise her singing and hope she would do a little dancing as well, but the lyrics draw a shadow over her face.

"What's the name of that song again?"

"Yoon Shimdeok sang it, 'Ode to Death.'"

"What a sorrowful song it is."

"Isn't it? Yoon Shimdeok recorded this song and did herself in with her lover."

"What does 'doing herself in' mean?"

"She killed herself."

Okkie says this like it were regular gossip about some neighbors, but her words deeply depress Juryong. Oblivious to her feelings, Okkie goes on talking about the incident.

"How deeply they must've loved each other to die together? I wish I could love like that someday."

"Love that's enough to die for is one thing, but why kill yourself over it?"

It's Jeonbin that Juryong is thinking about when she says this. Her tone makes Okkie turn a cautious gaze at Juryong for the first time. She must miss that husband she always talks about—Okkie's guess is correct. She changes the subject.

"Anything interesting happen at your factory, hyungnim?"

"Not really. What about you?"

"Well, I was punished by the foreman again. He spits out a lot of Japanese words whenever I get something wrong. I think they're insults, but I don't respond to it because I don't understand him."

Unlike the rubber factories, which were mostly established with Korean capital, the silk factories tended to have Japanese owners, even Japanese managers. Okkie's own factory had Korean spinners, but everyone from middle management upward is Japanese.

"How annoying for you."

"I'm fine. Listening to a few insults is nothing. The ones I really hate are the foolish girls who speak a little *nihongo* and go out of their way to be cute to get extra servings of rice. That's just unfair."

"A factory where you spin threads all day and you've got to speak Japanese too?"

"That's what I'm saying! A factory girl can speak ten languages and she still wouldn't be taken seriously."

They've arrived at their house. Okkie, despite insisting earlier that she's fine, angrily throws off her shoes and goes straight into Juryong's room. Like it's her own, Juryong thinks, grinning as she follows.

There was an aspect of life with Okkie that reminded her of her time with Jeonbin. Something to do with neither of them being relatives by blood but feeling like her closest family. Jeonbin was younger than her, like a sibling, and Okkie is just about young enough to be Juryong's daughter had she married early, but it has more to do with Okkie's age when she met her than their age difference.

Not long after Juryong had moved in, Okkie had had her first period. It was Juryong who gave Okkie her first menstrual rags, ones she had bought for herself but hadn't used yet. Okkie had almost thrown a tantrum at the thought of accidentally bleeding into her bedding overnight, which was why Juryong invited her to sleep in her room and how she came to practically live there. Having mistaken Okkie as a shy girl at first, Juryong did not mind how Okkie treated her like a long-lost older sister, and she came to be fond of her in return. Even if Juryong was closer in age to Okkie's mother, it was Okkie whom she thought of as a friend.

Okkie's mother, Lim, had given birth to her when she'd been around Okkie's age now. She was her first child and had lost two children who would've otherwise been Okkie's siblings. One died soon after childbirth and the other was stillborn. It was said they were buried in the hill behind the house. Okkie had two younger brothers, twins who were born not three years after Lim had buried her stillborn. That was when Okkie's grandmother, Lim's mother, passed away. After a lifetime of mocking her daughter as having no talents or fortune, the grandmother at least went to her death smiling happily at having seen two new grandsons at once.

Juryong was renting the room this grandmother had used. A factory worker in a similar situation as Juryong had lived in it before her, but this previous tenant had never allowed Okkie to sleep in her room. How happy it made Okkie, who had just started on her period, to sleep separately from her parents and her two eight-year-old brothers.

"Don't take this the wrong way, but if things go well for hyungnim and you move out, I'll get this whole room to myself!"

It tickled her fancy to say this, stroking the pictures of modern girls that Juryong had stuck to the walls using rice grains. Just like Juryong, it was Okkie's dream to be a modern girl someday. The girl has more potential to become one, thinks Juryong, she's young and she can be anything she wants to be.

"But don't you think you'll move out before I do?"

"Why would I move out of my own house?"

"Forget it. I'm just being stupid."

As realization hits Okkie, her perplexed expression turns into a sigh. This was a girl who was ostensibly going to the factories to save up for marriage. A point of pride on some occasions, one of despair in others. Okkie, who was proud to be earning not only her own keep but contributing to the tuition of her brothers. The same Okkie, to whom the thought of getting up at dawn every morning and working hard all day for the sake of mere marriage was abhorrent.

"I want to go to school."

Before her silk factory job, Okkie had spent a year at a girls' school. She learned to read Korean as well as division and multiplication.

"What's so good about school," retorts Juryong, "all you'll get is a headache."

Before Juryong left Pyongyang over ten years ago, she had lingered around the girls' school from summer to fall but had never got up the courage to say goodbye to her friends there before leaving for Gando.

"I want to become a proud modern girl later on and have free love with an intellectual, isn't that what they do in Choonwon's novels? You've got to be at least a high school graduate if you want to be a main character. I don't need to be the main character. I wish I'd at least graduated middle school."

Okkie's father scoffed at the notion of educating a daughter and forced her to drop out, sending only her brothers to school, who were now paying their tuition through her earnings. Renting out Juryong's room and farming some land, and with the mother and daughter both going to the factories, the family got by all right, but they saved every coin they had to send at least one of their sons through college.

Juryong is aware of what Okkie really wants. She doesn't want to spend the money she earns on marriage, she wants to spend it on an education.

"I want to live alone like hyungnim, too."

"I keep telling you, I don't live alone!"

An unreadable thought makes Okkie pout and frown with anger and frustration, but she soon sighs and grips Juryong's sleeve.

"I like you, hyungnim."

"And I like you too, Okkie."

"I wish we could live together forever."

Okkie's little hand gripping her sleeve looks so helpless and loving that Juryong comfortingly pats Okkie's shoulder with her other hand.

★

Okkie's whining in her sleep wakes Juryong in the night. Strands of hair on Okkie's forehead are drenched in sweat. Juryong wets a rag with water from a kettle and wipes Okkie's face before lying back down. She's glad she was awakened from a nightmare.

Juryong has recurring dreams of Gando these days. It's like watching a film of her own life. There she was, almost thirty and watching herself grow up in front of her, knowing full well what was about to befall the girl.

Juryong tries to talk to her. "Hey there, Kang girl. You'll be married soon. To the most handsome man you'll know. Kang girl, you're going to be a resistance fighter. Can you even imagine such a thing? Your husband will send you back home and die soon after. You'll be accused of murdering him and go to jail. The most ridiculous things will keep happening to you."

But the Kang girl in Juryong's dreams can't hear her. Just as no matter how loudly the audience talks to the cinema screen, the actors can't hear them either.

Sometimes, the dream doesn't go where it's supposed to go. Jeonbin doesn't die. Juryong doesn't get married. Fourteen-year-old Juryong doesn't go to Gando but remains in Pyongyang. Her family isn't ruined, and she gets to continue school. These dreams don't last long.

Because they've reached the limits of my imagination.

She's never thought of what she wanted to be when she grew up. All she did was live from day to day. Staying alive was hard, but wonderful sometimes. And survival kept her so busy she barely has time to reflect or think about what she wants for her future. No one taught her what to think, either.

Which is probably why she's still at the factory despite planning to quit as soon as enough money was saved to return to Gando. Choosing to stay in Pyongyang is perhaps not such a dramatic decision, but it's the first time she's made a choice purely for herself. Nothing like trying to decide whether to untie her hair before undressing or undressing before untying her hair. To follow her parents to the countryside, to get married because she was told to do so, to go with the resistance fighters because her husband was one of them, that had been her life up to this point. To do something just because she wanted to do it is a precious experience for her. Even if she knows there is little else she can do besides work at a rubber factory.

I hope you would get to do what you want, at least.

She gently strokes Okkie's hair one more time. Bold and bright, a little awkward at times and touchingly ordinary, this girl. She loves trends, craves learning. Wishes for the vaguest things without any wherewithal to attain them, a situation that often brings a pout of frustration to her face. Okkie frowns, she must be dreaming. Juryong sees the girl Kang in that face, a mirror into her own past.

★

"You're the hyungnim that lives with Okkie, aren't you?"

Juryong is suddenly surrounded by a group of young factory girls as she waits outside the gates for Okkie. They're much younger than her but taller, which instantly intimidates Juryong as they practically block out the sun. She tries to straighten her shoulders and nod, which elicits a burst of questions from the girls.

"Is it true you lived in Gando?"

"Did you really take part in the resistance movement?"

"And your husband was a resistance fighter?"

Juryong, momentarily overwhelmed, quickly regains her composure. "How do you girls know all this?"

The factory girls look at each other and smile. It's the smiles that make her feel uneasy.

"Is there a reason we shouldn't know? We just want to see if Okkie is lying or if she really has a friend who used to be a resistance fighter."

"You go to Pyongwon Rubber Factory, right? I have an aunt there, but she says she's never heard of you."

Over the shoulder of the tallest girl, Juryong finally spots Okkie at a distance, who seems to be hesitating as to whether to approach them or not. The girls keep babbling and Juryong keeps following Okkie with her gaze. After some hesitation, Okkie takes the long way around them.

"Oh hyungnim, do tell us. We're not asking hard questions, are we?"

Since leaving the resistance, she has no desire to talk about her time there. No one asks, and Juryong herself instinctively knows she needs to keep silent on the issue. She only told Okkie because she was so far away from Gando, and her husband who had brought her into the movement was dead, so who would care? Even if she leaped into a police station this minute and declared, "Hello gentlemen, I used to be a resistance fighter," all she would elicit would be laughter. Even Okkie occasionally questioned whether her stories were true. Which was why Juryong would tell them to her without a care if she was thought of as a liar. She did want to tell the stories someday, but not yet.

But all that was different from being fodder for gossip among strangers. Juryong never thought of her days in the resistance movement as heroic patriotism or anything very grand. Truth be told, there were a lot of embarrassing aspects to it. Especially since it was how she became a widow. Not even Okkie knew that Juryong had spent time in jail. Thinking about that time in her life still pained her as if it had happened yesterday.

Coming out of her thoughts, Juryong finally manages to get a word in.

"I don't know what Okkie's been saying to you, but don't you girls bully my Okkie."

The girls burst into laughter.

"Does it look like we would bully her? What would we possibly get out of doing that? That little girl has less than nothing."

The careless words have a sharpness that find their way into Juryong's heart.

"You really should be angry at her, hyungnim. She's got nothing of her own to brag about, so she's using you instead."

Juryong stands speechless as the girls move on toward the dorms, chattering among themselves.

All the way back home she feels an inexplicable anger as she goes over what the girls had said to her. They were right. Okkie wants to be special but there isn't anything different about her compared to the other factory girls. Even the fact that she wants to stand out is the same. Okkie must've gossiped about all the things she told her, the things she said the other day as well. To call a general of the resistance fighters Gwangwoon-ssi like he was some neighbor, what a casual boast that would've been. Vainly blabbering on about Juryong's story, a story Juryong had told to assuage her sadness at hearing of the passing of someone she had once depended so much on. How was she to punish this girl?

The house feels strange. The dog's not barking, well, that's not so unusual, but the lights are all off. Not even the lamplight is on. She opens her door and finds the room empty. There are whispers coming from the master bedroom. Okkie's father must be chiding Okkie. The thought exhausts Juryong. What could he possibly say to a girl refusing to come over to Juryong's room because she was afraid of being scolded by Juryong?

For days she tries to find a chance to talk to the girl. Okkie would retire to the master bedroom immediately after finishing her supper, and she who had once been so reluctant to wake up early is now the first to leave the house at the crack of dawn. It's almost as if they don't live in the same house.

Since being accosted by the factory girls, Juryong finds it hard to tamp down her anger—but after a little while, it seems foolish to be angry over what a young girl had done. She hates the thought of being talked about, but that doesn't mean Juryong and Okkie have to fall out forever because of it, or to cut each other out of their lives when they'd shared their deepest secrets.

About two weeks later, right before Chuseok, Okkie knocks on Juryong's door, after Juryong has waited for so long and tried so hard to talk to her, burning through her frustration.

And here she finally is, that little creature.

Letting her wait a bit, Juryong finally opens the door, suppressing a smile. But as soon as she does so, Okkie says something unexpected.

"Hyungnim, after Chuseok, I'm supposed to go into the dorms."

Her hand still gripping the door handle, Juryong swallows her shock before replying.

"Is that all you have to say to me?"

Okkie doesn't answer.

★

On the day of Chuseok, the factories lie silent.

Juryong stands on the road leading into downtown. Okkie will come down it once she's back from ancestral rites.

It's hard to resist thoughts of the past on holidays. The tables they would carefully lay out for the rites in Gando. The rice cakes they managed to make, frugally shoring up every little bit of nothing they had. The chestnuts they had saved for later and the taste of dust when they finally bring themselves to eat them, the ear-brightening wine one tiredly paces in circles behind the houses to have a taste of, the stew cooked with not pheasant or chicken but rabbit. The faces in these scenes. Family.

Okkie appears with her hair neatly slicked back with water and tied into a braid.

"Did you wait long?"

"No. Let's go."

The weather isn't too cold to walk but Juryong has crossed her arms as if her hands are freezing. Hating to see Okkie with her head bowed and nervously fidgeting with her fingers, she keeps looking away.

It was Juryong who proposed today's walk. Not that they would never see each other again once Okkie moves into the dorm, but she feels sorry and uneasy that she's the reason Okkie had decided to move, Juryong wants to make one more memory that Okkie could look back on someday. Although she does wonder now if there's a point to any of it.

"Okkie, have you been to the Eulmildae?"

"Not since I was little."

Having walked in silence up to the Daedong Bridge that arches over the river, Okkie shuffles up to Juryong and hooks her hand in the crook of Juryong's arm.

"Are you afraid of heights?"

"A bit."

"Want to ride a boat across instead?"

"Oh, hyungnim. Let's just take the bridge."

Whether it's because of the holiday or they're passing the busiest part of Pyongyang, they are met with crowds of people. It's not easy dragging a fearful Okkie through them, and a few pedestrians curse as they shove past. But this isn't so bad. Juryong slows her pace to match her companion's.

The Daedong Bridge didn't exist when Juryong lived here as a child. To be able to walk across the river on foot, what a wonderful world it is—Okkie's lack of conversation leaves plenty of room for such silly thoughts. Juryong also hadn't been up to the Eulmildae Pagoda since she was a child. Thinking she could go any time, she never got around to it.

"Should we go up there now?"

On Eulmilbong peak on Geumsusan Mountain, a pagoda was constructed on a strut at least ten meters high—this was the Eulmildae Pagoda. The pagoda has the best view in the city, but they can already see crowds waiting below for their turn.

Okkie shakes her head. "The view from here isn't so bad, either."

Well, if she fears heights so much that crossing a bridge makes her afraid, there's no way she's going up that mountain. Juryong fans at the beads of sweat on her face as they walk around the strut. Okkie follows a step or two behind as if she hadn't stuck right by Juryong's side on the bridge a moment before.

Juryong shouts over the crowd, "Anything you'd like to eat?"

Okkie's answer is hesitant. "I want to try coffee."

In the cafe, Okkie looks as bewildered as when Juryong had her first cup of coffee. Instead of sitting for a bit to chat, Okkie swallows all her coffee in one go like it's medicine, which means they have to get up almost as soon as they sit down. And when Juryong pays, Okkie's face blanches at the price, just as Juryong's had.

As casually as Juryong had been about the café and the bill, it had only been a few months since Juryong's own first coffee, and she's only drunk a couple of more cups compared to her young friend. Secretly, she had hoped Okkie wouldn't realize that. She wanted Okkie to keep looking up to her. But how was this vanity different from Okkie's, who had merely wanted to stand out among the other girls at the factory? If only she had been more thoughtful with Okkie and shared her feelings more. They take a ferry back across the river to their neighborhood.

As Okkie drags her feet back to her family's room, Juryong stops her. "Sleep in my room, just for tonight."

A moment of indecision. Okkie obliges.

Inside, Juryong presents Okkie with a package in a boja-gi wrap.

"Try these on," she says as she unwraps it.

Unaware of Okkie's exact measurements, Juryong had chosen a pair that were slightly smaller than her own size. Okkie stares down at them for a while before slowly fitting them on her own feet.

"They're just right," says Okkie.

It's a lie. She had to pinch them in the back and really stuff her feet. I should've given her larger ones, thinks Juryong sadly, if only because she's still a growing girl. She swallows these words. The shoes remind her of the ones her mother bought her for her wedding. Wherever they were now, they had fit her feet perfectly, not even a little bit too big or small. Why was her silly mind thinking back to those shoes? Juryong furtively presses down on the sobs that threaten to surface.

"Hyungnim, I'm so sorry."

"What's there to be sorry for?"

"I told your stories without your permission, and I didn't say I was sorry before now . . ."

"If you're really sorry, you won't move into the dorms."

"I've already promised, I can't."

"I know. I had to try just once. Don't worry about it."

Sighing, Juryong spreads the bedding. Fidgeting still, Okkie sits down on it.

"Hyungnim, you know I'm not leaving for good."

"I know. Let's go to sleep early tonight."

"I'm sorry."

"Stop saying you're sorry, there's nothing to be sorry for."

Juryong stretches out on the bedding.

"Sing me a song, Okkie."

Okkie hesitates for a moment before singing the Yoon Shim-deok song. Her voice quivers with tears.

In this lonely world full of harsh suffering
What are you looking for...

She can't finish the song.

During the night, Juryong feels Okkie get up from her side. She pretends to turn her back to her in her sleep, waiting for Okkie to leave. Okkie stands there a moment longer before gently tucking the quilt around Juryong's shoulders, and she is gone.

Juryong turns back to Okkie's side and feels the spot on the bedding where Okkie had lain. The slight depression there is flattened by the stroke of her palm.

I've lost another friend.

Strangely, she feels nothing as she brings her hand to her chest. Just the bones there below her neck. The shape of her ribs makes her feel that something is caged within her.

3

ANYONE WHO DOESN'T WORK CAN GO HOME

There's a horizontal banner on the wall of the neighboring factory. Juryong stops in her tracks on the way to work and slowly reads out the words.

"Anyone... who... doesn't... work..."

What a silly thing to write on a banner, of course anyone who doesn't work should go home. But it soon occurs to her that the banner must be addressing the strikes being organized across the country. Juryong nods to herself as she makes the connection.

The striking workers do not go home. They linger around their factories, shouting their demands. Juryong hasn't joined a union, and none of the other workers in her section have, either. Sometimes they talk about unionizing, but the managers would come prowling around the corner and they would fall silent—and that was that.

At Juryong mentioning the slogan, the woman Hong makes it clear that she doesn't think much of the strike action.

"All these strikes," she says, "what's the point if the machines end up rusting? Someone has to keep the motors running if they want to have jobs to come back to. They just have nothing to do in their factories. Even in our own factory, what was it, the Great Depression? We had so little work then. Some girls would get work all month and others maybe three times a week, and none of us could save any money. And sometimes, no one would go to work. Now that there's no work and a strike, the factory owners must be pleased, they don't have to pay anyone."

Hong seems to have a point. Strike or not, it looks more like people killing time to her. But doesn't Hong have grievances against the management herself?

"Then what would you do in their place, Hong hyungnim?"

"If I were a factory owner, I would fire the lot of them and hire new workers."

"A true-born factory owner you are, hyungnim."

It was one thing for a skilled master like Hong to not worry about getting fired, but what about the apprentices who had barely a year's worth of experience under their belts? As other factories were facing their own troubles, moving jobs would be impossible. At least the male workers in the mixing team, rollers team, or administrative staff had guaranteed jobs just for being men, and management were reluctant to dismiss breadwinners. But the women, they could be dismissed at will just like Hong had said. The factory women—who normally would be whispering to each other—are hard at work with nary a peep, as if fearing for their jobs. The foreman, who usually goes around stirring up trouble, also stays in his place these days.

Their workday is cut short again. At some point, the factory unceremoniously got rid of free lunches and began sending the workers home instead. Then the factory owner, whom they had never so much as glimpsed in previous times, comes down to the factory floor, gathers the workers in one place, and makes a speech. He hadn't done that even when a wage cut was declared. It's annoying enough that their workday has been cut short, and now they're prevented from going home early to attend to urgent housework, just for the sake of his silly speech. He tells them that workers are now forbidden from gathering in groups of more than three, and anyone breaking this rule would be punished.

"What on earth is he saying," Hong mutters, "if four factory workers walk down the corridor arm in arm, he's going to call the police or something? Once I'm out of the gates, I'm a free woman."

Hong's voice is quite loud considering how she declared, just this morning, that disobedient workers should be fired. As they walk out of the factory, Hong defiantly slinks her arms into Juryong and Ginseng's on either side of her. Counting the baby Ginseng has slung to her chest, that's four people.

"Even when we go to the bathroom we go in threes or fours, so what's he going to do about that?"

"He's afraid we're going to start unionizing if we gather in more than threes," Juryong says mockingly, trying to keep her voice light.

The groups of workers leaving the factory collapse into laughter.

"But is our factory really the only one that's not going on strike?"

"What, you want us to stop working too?"

"That other rubber factory over there, they kept talking about it, everyone needs to go on strike, everyone needs to act as one!"

This is from Ginseng, mimicking the voice coming from the empty lot near the factories where there's a gathering every morning.

"But isn't it good for us if everyone else strikes and we keep working? Our wages keep falling as it is, we should be grabbing what hours we can."

"That's not true at all! It's better for us to make factory owners accept our demands instead of doing everything they're telling us to do."

This last bit comes from someone from behind the woman Hong. Judging from her appearance, she must be one of those strikers at the nearby sit-in site. Tired and shabby, her eyes still flash with fire, making her look a little off-kilter, but also giving her an irresistible look of boldness.

Hong, eyes narrowed in suspicion, coils her arms around Ju-ryong and Ginseng's even tighter.

"What demands? And since when was I a part of this 'us' you're talking about?"

"*Us* means all of us laborers. Can you really say you have nothing to demand from the factory owners?"

"Well, if they give me my money on time and don't hit me, that's all I ask for."

"That's what we're asking for as well. A stable income and to be treated respectfully. And paid maternity leave," she adds looking at the child Ginseng is holding, "which means you get your salary even when you're resting at home after having a baby. These are all a part of our demands."

"Having a baby is a family affair," says Ginseng as she adjusts her hold on the baby, "how could I charge money for work I'm not doing?"

"But those are our rights, and it is us who are ignorant of them."

"Let's go," Hong says, "she's trying to con us."

She pulls at Juryong and Ginseng like a yoked ox. But neither wants to move.

The union member smiles.

"You were let off work early, right? Follow me. Gladly I will tell you our rights and what we hope to win from the strike."

★

In the tent, there are about fifty people sitting on the floor. A few male workers here and there, but mostly factory women like Juryong. The rows of factory women in white jeogori tunics and black skirts are like rice balls wrapped in dried seaweed. Imagining the foreman finding them sitting here makes Juryong shudder.

"I need to go to the toilets," says Hong as she backs away.

The woman who brought them here grabs her sleeve. "Why don't I show you where the toilets are?"

"Never mind. It's gone back in."

Her escape plan thwarted, Hong reluctantly sits down. The sight of the well-worn straw mat, sat and stepped on so many times that Juryong could see the ground beneath it, makes her wonder what she's doing here; as Hong dusts off a spot for the other two to sit, the crowd begins to clap.

A woman has stepped up on the podium made from an upturned wooden box.

"Thank you for coming, comrades! My name is Kang Deoksam of the Pyongyang Laborers' Union."

The word *comrades* sends a thrill through Juryong's heart. She could hardly remember the last time she was called comrade.

"Today we have comrades who have just joined the strike, comrades who have attended many educational sessions but want to hear it one more time, and others who have no intention of participating in the strike. All are welcome today. All we ask of you is to understand why the strike is important. We've already declared our plans to hold a strike, and so far, 2,300 comrades working in rubber factories in Pyongyang are ready to come together as one and fight for our rights."

Were there really 2,300 women working in rubber factories in Pyongyang? The number alone makes Juryong's heart thump loudly.

"Those who agree with what we say today, please press your thumbprint to an application form we have here. Again, you don't have to join. We already know what determination and bravery you needed to have to even come here. And are we not all comrades? Everyone who is a laborer is a comrade!"

Kang Deoksam receives another round of applause as she vacates the podium for a man wearing round glasses. Self-consciously, the man pushes his spectacles up his nose as he looks around him. The durumagi robe he is wearing, once black, is so worn that it's the color of ash. Kang Deoksam, who had gone on before him, was a factory woman like them, and her friendly yet firm way of address had immediately inspired admiration—this man, an obvious intellectual, is amusing in his awkwardness, even before he opens his mouth.

Someone drags a poster hanger onto the stage, the kind Juryong had seen as a child in school. A welcome sight that makes her jab Hong with her elbow and grin. Hong makes a show of shoving her elbow, but she doesn't seem as eager to make her escape as before. Suppressing the laughter this sight inspires in her, Juryong looks over at Ginseng seated on the other side of Hong, hoping to get her to tease Hong as well, but Ginseng is enraptured by the presentation.

The story begins with the Great Depression that had swept the world some years before. The man turns the posters on the hanger as he speaks, eventually moving on to the union's demands. Just as the union member who had brought them here said, they include paid maternity leave. Juryong sneaks a look at Ginseng and Hong from time to time. Tears well in Ginseng's eyes. Even as she turns to give her whining baby her breast, she never lets the podium out of her sight. In the tent, there are about ten other women like Ginseng who are carrying babies.

After the educational session is over, the strike organizers pass out applications for the union. Ginseng's hand shoots up in the air. Stamping her thumbprint hard on the application, she goes as far as to make a speech. As she gets on the podium with her baby in her arms, she receives the loudest applause of all the speakers so far.

"All this time," she says loudly, "I took it for granted that if I had a baby and didn't go out to work, I would not get paid. But today's session taught me that if the factory owner had guaranteed paid maternity leave, I never would've had to go work when I was at death's door. I could've come back when I was stronger, and I would've worked even harder!"

The applause makes her too shy to continue for a moment. Tears are flowing down her face. Since having the baby, Juryong observes, Ginseng has cried often. Ginseng hugs the baby hard as the applause dies down.

"I also learned today that you have to go down to the fourteenth or so demand to get to the part about maternity leave. Aside from that little disappointment, I think I gained a lot today. I am determined to obtain maternity leave by the time I have my second child!"

★

Ginseng had started working in the factory as soon as she got married, and she kept having trouble conceiving. Hong claimed that Ginseng's irregular periods meant having a child would be difficult, and Juryong, who'd never had children herself, nevertheless nodded along. The stench of cooking rubber would make Ginseng nauseous, which would make all the other women give her expectant looks, but she only shook her head. "If this keeps up he'll take a concubine," Ginseng would joke.

Not on the nothing your husband brings in, Juryong almost retorts, but she pounds her chest in frustration instead.

The only person in Ginseng's house earning any money is Ginseng. Her husband's older sisters have all been married off, which means as the only son it's her husband's obligation to take care of his old mother, but it's not as if he does housework or has a job. The bridal money he had given to Ginseng's family had made her think she was marrying a well-off family, but it turned out that money had been their last bit of capital. She'd been bought with what amounted to less than an ox's worth. While made to breed and work like an ox.

The dark despair during the days after her wedding when she first learned of the truth of her circumstances made life at the factory a reprieve if anything. Much better than being hen-pecked and nagged by her mother-in-law and husband, neither of whom did anything all day. At the factory at least, she had work and peers.

Despite her bringing in money and doing all the housework on top of it, her mother-in-law had chastised her for not getting pregnant. Even if children were something Ginseng also wanted for the family, it galls the way her mother-in-law berates her. A year into their marriage, the husband brought up the prospect of bringing in a concubine like it was nothing. Ginseng related this with a laugh.

"Do you think," she wondered aloud, "he'll use the money I bring in to buy another woman? Let him do that, but why should he say it like he's doing it because of me, blaming me for it? As if that wasn't what he had always wanted to do in the first place?"

About four months after her last period, Ginseng couldn't help hoping this was it. She only wanted to tell Juryong and Hong, her closest friends at the factory, but once Hong knew, so did everyone else. Hong rubbed Ginseng's belly and encouragingly said, "How firm it is, you're sure to be pregnant now." When Ginseng fretted aloud about the factory and housework and whether the baby will keep through all that, Hong reassuringly gripped her hand saying, "The baby knows Mother works at a rubber factory, the baby will be sticky like rubber and stick to Mother, you'll see, all my babies turned out fine."

Only at about seven months did Ginseng start to show. Having pummeled and harassed her like always up until then, the foreman stopped hitting her, perhaps scared of what would happen if he made her lose the baby.

Ginseng clocked in for work, even at nine months pregnant, for every day except when the factory was closed. When she failed to meet her quota by a few pairs, the others took turns making it up for her with their extras. Not that such days were common.

Four days after her water broke right after she had arrived at work, Ginseng returned to the factory a shadow of her former self. She had wanted to come back as soon as possible but having been in labor for a whole day and night, her body refused to cooperate for days afterward. Every joint in her body hurt like teeth biting down on tinfoil, but she still had to carry the baby in one arm and handle the rubber molds with the other. Neither her miserable mother-in-law or husband could be trusted to take care of the baby at home, and if she quit her job, they would have nothing to eat. An infuriating situation, but Hong said there were many women with similar circumstances. While Juryong worried over Ginseng and the baby at having to live like this, Hong simply shook her head and said this was Ginseng's fate to bear.

A year has passed, and the baby is now one.

Ginseng, sometimes, would be caught crying by herself. When her eyes meet Juryong's, Ginseng would shake her head, saying that she wasn't sad or sorrowful, she just seems to have broken the plumbing when she had her baby, and that because the child is a daughter, her husband already wants to try for a son. Ginseng says this with a smile, with tears still running down her face.

★

Another shortened workday. Juryong and Ginseng talk to a few of the other workers and bring them to the strike tent. Hong, complaining all the way, follows them inside. The tent is more crowded than ever. Like Juryong has done, the people from yesterday have managed to convince some of their coworkers to join them.

"All of these factories are cutting their hours short? Are they asking us to unionize and strike or what?"

At Kang Samdeok's joke, delivered on the podium as soon as she introduced herself, the audience bursts into laughter.

From then on, Juryong visits the strike headquarters tent every day her hours are cut or the factory is closed. She bumps into other workers she isn't that close to. But even coming in every day, she's reluctant to hand in an application. Ginseng had put her thumbprint on the paperwork on her first day, as well as the workers they brought to the tent, and even Hong, who had been so adamantly against it at first, had handed in her form—but Juryong still hesitates. She doesn't know why. Feeling passionate and fired up during the educational sessions is one thing, but she keeps wondering if it is indeed wise to jump into something new so wholeheartedly.

Four days before the scheduled general strike, the factory owner comes down to deliver another talk, saying that there are reports of workers falling prey to ideological garbage, vowing that this shall not be tolerated at this factory, and more words of that nature.

"What a load of lies," says Juryong, "I hope he slips in the outhouse and falls head-first into shit."

Ginseng doesn't laugh at the colorful image Juryong paints as they leave the factory gates. Bereft of the laughter she had expected from her, Juryong grabs hold of Ginseng's arm and talks in a deliberately light manner.

"What can they possibly do to us? Bore us to death like today, or scare us again?"

Ginseng, her face still dark, gently takes her arm out of Juryong's grip.

"Ryong-ah, I'm going to quit the union."

What's all this about?

"I told my husband last night. That I wanted to participate in the strike so we would have a better future. Because he was going on and on about me coming home late, even with reduced work hours. I had no choice. He screamed at me about what the newspapers were saying about the strike."

"What an ignorant fool he is. It is the duty of educated people like us to be generous and forgiving of people like him."

Juryong's attempt at mirth only results in Ginseng's sobs. As often as she cried nowadays, Juryong senses these tears are different.

"But you see," says Ginseng, "the factory is already refusing to tolerate us. They sent some administrative workers to our house yesterday and asked if the housewife was also taking part in the strike. That if I did take part in the strike, they would fire me, and then my husband threatened to divorce me if that happened. He really threatened me!"

Juryong feels sorry for Ginseng, who bursts into tears at this point, but it's hard not to scoff at what she has just said.

"What a ridiculous notion! You might as well just divorce him. Does he really think there's another person in that household besides you who is a real adult? Who does he think will really benefit from a divorce, him or you?"

"But if that happens, I'm afraid he'll take away my baby. And everyone will mock me for being the woman who got divorced for striking."

The things you worry about, Juryong almost says, but stops herself. People look down at her all the time for being a young widow, and she is always careful not to stand out in a crowd because of it. As she tries to search for words to comfort Ginseng, the younger woman continues to cry.

"I've only been a member for a less than a month, it's embarrassing to quit now, but I'm earning money for my family, and now I'm scared that if I insist on my rights, I'll lose that very family. What am I going to do? I don't know what to do!"

"Come on, keep it together, what on earth did you have for breakfast that you're crying so much? Look at me. Come on, look at me."

Juryong grips Ginseng's shoulders tight as Ginseng effortfully fixes her watery gaze on Juryong.

"If you leave the union, I'll join instead. Doesn't that sound like a good idea? I'll go in your stead and see this labor activist business to the very end."

"What difference does it make if one person goes in while another goes out?"

"A big difference. Because I'm not going to be an ordinary member. Ginseng, do you know why I kept putting off joining? Because knowing me, I would devote my whole life to the cause if I joined, which is why I didn't until now. I can't keep putting it off when you're about to leave as well. I'm going into the union because of you, you're the one who's making me join."

Ginseng stops her crying. Juryong keeps talking, not knowing what's going to come out of her own mouth next.

"So it's not like one person joining when one person leaves. Because it's not just one person joining. I am going to do the work of a thousand people, and thanks to you Ginseng, a thousand people just joined the strike. Do you understand?"

Whatever it is to be understood, Ginseng nods. She still looks a bit perplexed by the situation. Juryong, still on a high, grabs Ginseng's wrist and brings her into the tent.

"May I have an application form and a resignation form?"

The union officer is amused she is asking for not one of the two but both. As she fills in the form and stamps her thumbprint, Juryong keeps an eye on Ginseng's face. She has also stamped her leave form and is looking at Juryong, who shakes the form, drying her thumbprint, and grins.

Today the educational session is led by the branch leader of a nearby silk factory, delivering what is called a declaration of solidarity. Juryong holds on tight to Ginseng's hand and thinks of Okkie as she listens. A branch leader she may be, but the worker is a girl, at most only a couple of years older than Okkie.

"Unlike the rubber factories," this worker says in a clear voice, "most of the silk factories are run with Japanese capital. In other words, we at the silk factories are largely young girls like me and, with the slightest sign of unrest being trampled down by the Japanese police, it's doubly hard to make any kind of resistance against the owners. But no matter how young we are, we know the value of our labor, and we know it's wrong for them to work us more than the previous month but pay us less, to promise us education and housing and end up charging for our education and the dorms, and to provide us with rice that's mixed with rat droppings. Skin infections and malnutrition send our comrades to hospitals by the hundreds, and their favorite way of justifying this poor treatment is to say we're going to quit the silk factory to work at the rubber factory when we're married anyway. And that because our work isn't skilled, they can replace us at any time."

When the rubber factory is mentioned, there's a burst of applause from the audience. While unsure if the moment deserves it, Juryong claps along.

"That's right. We know very well that the life of a rubber factory woman is our future. What else is a factory girl to become, other than another factory girl? Which is why my comrades here before me, each and every hyungnim, is our future. Your victory is our victory, which is why the silk factory workers will band together to support your strike!"

Another burst of cheers and applause. This time, Juryong's clapping is enthusiastic. It shames her to think that a moment ago, she too thought fleetingly that this young woman would simply get married and disappear. The fact that she understood Juryong's situation and is fighting for her rights at such a young age means the girl is the better person, if anything. Why hadn't she realized until this moment that to join the strike with all her dedication and passion was not only to help herself but Ginseng and Okkie as well?

Next came time for the new members to introduce themselves. Juryong raises both her hands immediately, and even before they call on her, she strides up to the podium.

"Hello, comrades! My name is Kang Juryong, and I work in the Pyongwon Rubber Factory. I joined so I can be the next head of the Pyongyang Rubber Workers Union!"

A moment of silence. Then, a burst of laughter and applause. Among the smiling faces is Ginseng's, which shines with extra joy. Juryong suddenly feels shy, but she speaks as confidently as she possibly can.

"To be honest, there was nothing more I wanted to be than a modern girl. No, if I were being truly honest, I still haven't lost that dream. But now, my wish is to lead this strike!"

What is she going on about, the crowd seems to think as their laughter grows louder. They probably think she's a late convert, a born-again activist full of herself, or some vain attention hog.

"Why are you laughing? Is there a law against factory girls from becoming modern girls? My foreman thinks the same way, he grabbed me by the hair and beat me for having such thoughts when I started at my factory. He told me that modern girls were either students or whores. He even said that if I wanted to prove I was a modern girl, I should have free love with him!

"I know my only education is the education I've been given here, but that education has been enough! Enough for me to realize that modern girls are not better or more important than factory girls, enough for me to know that we are equals! That whether a factory girl dreams of being a modern girl, the foreman had no right to treat me the way he did!"

The crowd has grown silent. Then, someone begins to clap. A few people join in, and then more. Juryong waits for the thunderous applause to die down as she suppresses the sobs welling up in her throat.

"Today I have joined, and today a comrade of mine who works right by my side had to leave the movement. Do you know why, comrades? Our factory owner sent people to her house and made her husband threaten her with divorce if she went on strike."

"They did that to me, too!"

"Me also!"

The shouts are coming from all over the place. Juryong glimpses Ginseng sobbing.

"They don't think of us as people! If we want to show them that we're people, and that we are more powerful people than they are, we have to show them a unified front using this strike. I may be a mere beginner and the things I learned in this tent the only education I have, but I want to say this one more time: I, Kang Juryong, will stand and lead this strike!

"And I promise to fight to the death for my comrades, and for myself!"

4

The general strike rally is like a festival. Wearing slogans written on sashes with a flourish, they march toward the factory zone, accompanied by union members dressed in sadangpae colors and playing drums brought from who knows where. Not to mention the bicycle-drawn cart where union officers take turns standing on and shouting slogans.

Factory owners capitulate!
Victory through workers' unity!
If those who do not work must starve
Then capitalists must starve!

Juryong rushes up to the cart and asks, "What does the slogan you just shouted mean?"

"It's from the book that the Jesus followers carry around. It means you only get as many rights as the time you've put in."

"Thank you for explaining it!"

Juryong thinks about the slogan hung by the factories: ANY-ONE WHO DOESN'T WORK CAN GO HOME. The factory owners, the capitalists must've taken that from the same book. When it's they themselves who were the ones not working—what hypocrisy!

"Let us now sing 'The Internationale!'"

Beginning with the prompt, *Inter-inter-internationale*, the union begins singing "The Internationale" as they were taught during the educational sessions:

'Tis the final conflict
Let each stand in his place
The international working class
Shall be the human race

To hear hundreds singing the song normally mumbled through in the tent by only a few while learning the lyrics, Juryong's heart swells. That so many people can gather to sing the same words, that they become one at least while they sing this single song. They say that "The Internationale" was sung by laborers not just in Korea but all over the world—when she sings it, Juryong no longer feels like she's a pitiful factory woman in a small factory in a small country, but a laborer standing equally arm in arm with all the other laborers across the world.

The next song is "The Eldest Daughter at the Rubber Factory." There are those who hadn't learned "The Internationale" by heart yet, but everyone knows this song. Anyone from Pyongyang, that is.

At the sound of the commuter bus engine gunning
The eldest daughter at the rubber factory packs her lunch
Sitting all day piecing shoes together
She pieces them prettily so she will be a pretty bride one day

Her tears finally fall. But because they're not from sorrow, she isn't ashamed of them. And she is hardly the only person crying.

They march around the factory zone and return to the empty lot where they started. Kang Deoksam and the officers of the

Pyongyang Laborers Union rubber industry division go up to the podium and make speeches. Fliers about the strike circulate. Both printed and copied by hand, they detail how 1,500 factory workers from about ten factories around the city are participating in the strike, as well as a list of the major slogans and the strikers' twenty demands.

Juryong feels the thrill of anticipated victory. It is said that about a thousand factory workers are gathered there, surely if each of them went around punching a factory owner in the face, their skulls wouldn't last by the end of the day? This silly fantasy makes her cackle to herself.

After the strikers are dismissed, she makes her way home on lighter feet. Even if there's a negotiation, it's impossible to know how long the factory owners would take in accepting the demands, and they had to survive without a salary until then; once the demands were met, though, work conditions would be much better than they are now, so it was all right. And it surely wouldn't be long now.

When she arrives home, there is a man she has never met standing in the yard. Thick-rimmed glasses, short-sleeved dress shirt, trousers with suspenders, and oxblood enamel shoes. Is he lost? He contrasts so much with Okkie's house that it makes her tilt her head. A friend of Okkie's father, perhaps? The dog, ever silent in the presence of strangers, paces the yard as it keeps an eye on the man.

"Excuse me. I am here to see someone named Kang Juryong. Is this the right address?"

Juryong, who is about to go into her room, stops in her tracks. "And why are you looking for Kang Juryong?"

The man looks down at a piece of paper he's holding and up at the house and Juryong. "I heard Kang was part of the Pyongyang rubber laborers' strike—"

"Are you police?"

At Juryong's sharp question, the man seems disconcerted, then grins. "Well, not police, I just want to meet Kang Juryong. But not to make an arrest."

"I'm Kang Juryong," she says boldly. She's never been so impertinent in introducing herself before. The man stares at her face then laughs.

"Your name made me think you would be a man."

"And what makes you so high and mighty that you laugh at the mention of someone else's name?"

Juryong's iciness makes the man stop laughing and clear his throat.

"Please excuse me, my name is Jeong Dalhon. I study labor unions at the Korean Communist Party."

"Surely a labor union is something that one does, not studies?"

Juryong's suspicion-laden answer makes Dalhon burst into even louder laughter than when he realized Kang Juryong was a woman.

"How right you are, and your name and your character are truly heroic. Just as I was told."

"Do not mock someone's name. The *Ju* stands for everywhere, the *Ryong* stands for dragon. I am to be the dragon that embraces the entire world." It was Jeonbin who had come up with this story behind her name.

Dalhon clears his throat. "I am sorry, this is not why I came here."

"Then state your business and leave. I don't want any passersby to get the wrong idea."

"Ah, yes. Your husband might misunderstand this situation."

Juryong opens her eyes wide and stares at Dalhon.

What a talent this man has for saying exactly the wrong thing! It's my fault, he's dressed like an intellectual and that made me curious about what he has to say, I never should've bothered.

"I don't know what you heard about me before coming to see me, but I don't think I have anything more to say to the likes of you."

"Look here, I am in a difficult situation myself. Someone had told me there was a promising potential organizer at a factory that has yet to have a union, and here I am, meeting that person and finding out she is a woman! Wouldn't you find that surprising?"

"Then you should stop wasting your time with some worthless woman and go study your unions, why don't you?" Juryong goes right into her room as Dalhon looks on, still standing in the yard.

"I am here to create a union," he says, "not study it. With you, Juryong-ssi."

"I already have an affiliation," Juryong says through the door, "I'm not interested. Go ask someone else."

Silence. Is he gone? She cracks open the door, and there is no one there. On the one hand she's glad none of Okkie's family had to see that wretched scene, but on the other it had been such an unexpected interlude that she wishes there had been another witness.

Even as she lay in bed to sleep that night, she is still fuming over the intellectual who had so offended her that afternoon. What could she have said that would've brought him to his knees?

But she has to admit that it was probably beyond her to win an argument of wits against an intellectual.

★

After the rally, Juryong visits the strike headquarters every day, listening to the news before walking back home.

Dailies, weeklies, it doesn't matter what newspaper—they all criticize the strike. The steam of the rally has evaporated, and exhaustion shows in everyone's face.

The factory owners haven't responded at all to their demands. A planned speech rally against them is broken up by the police, who keep exerting pressure on the strike organizers. The strike is already breaking apart at the seams.

But Juryong still believes in victory.

Because the rubber factories were established through Korean capital and the police are more intent on protecting Japanese interests, the latter had rarely bothered with labor union issues. But the police are paying attention now because they've determined that this movement has the potential to unite all the laborers of Pyongyang, regardless of industry.

There are now almost 2,000 factory workers participating in the strike.

Among them are numerous wives under threat of divorce like Ginseng, but they have no desire to turn away from the heat of the general strike. Workers from nearby factories in different industries drop off homemade rice wine on their way to work, even donating collections they've taken up for the rubber workers' cause.

Newspaper criticisms hold little meaning for them. They're just some chicken scratches scribbled by some idiot who knows how to sit down at a desk with a pen. Juryong can still hear the applause and shouts from the crowds lining their march.

Small things gather to make big things possible—Juryong still believes this. She believes the strikers will win.

★

Dalhon reappears at her house four days after the first day she met him, or four days after the rally. This time, Juryong speaks to him first.

"I'm very sure I told you once before that I'm not interested in whatever activity you're proposing."

"Why do you say that as if we've actually talked about anything?" says Dalhon with a sigh. He's fanning himself with a leaflet. It is August. How long had he been waiting in this heat?

Juryong beats down the sympathy she's beginning to feel for him and spits out, "Who taught you to go running after women in their homes? And who gave you my address? Whoever it was, why didn't they bother telling you that the woman who lives at that address is a pitiful widow?"

"Why didn't you say so before? I would have apologized immediately if you had. I know this is long overdue, but please forgive me. In my attempt to mind my manners, I have ended up causing you great offense instead."

In the face of his apology, Juryong is at a loss for words.

"I have this acquaintance," Dalhon continues, "an organizer of the educational sessions at your strike headquarters. She told me there was a member named Kang Juryong who was good-natured and bold, who declared everyone a comrade on the day she joined the strikers."

He must've seen her address in her application form. Juryong nods at this realization. And his words, while not enough to dispel her disgust, are also not unpleasant to hear.

"I think," he says, "my acquaintance told me about you thinking it were obvious you were a woman, and I heard your name and simply assumed you were a man. That is truly my fault. I am sorry."

"All right. But I really do think you should stop coming to look for me at my home. The whole neighborhood will begin talking about the widow who keeps bringing strange men into her room."

"Until you promise to work with me, I have no choice but to come here and beg you."

"Surely I'm not the only rubber factory worker in all of Pyongyang? There's already a union and we're in the middle of a strike, what can there possibly be for me to do?"

"This strike will fail. We have to prepare for what comes after. And we're not only talking to you, Juryong-ssi. Other factory workers from all over are being organized. But I have a good feeling about you. Is it not true you declared upon joining that you will become the head of the Pyongyang rubber workers' union? Does that answer your question?"

The only thing Juryong heard properly in Dalhon's answer is the first line.

"You think we will fail in our strike?"

Juryong looks poised to hit him, and Dalhon's hands and eyebrows go up in a defensive posture.

"It's the police," he explains, "we have a chance at winning some of the demands, but most of the leadership involved in this strike are sure to be arrested…"

Juryong's two fists, with nowhere to go, are shaking in the air. "It is unjust that people are jailed just for participating in a strike!"

"The current strike has no guarantee of the right of assembly. Which is why the last demand on the list is for the right to assemble. Absurd, of course. The right to assemble should not be anyone's right to give in the first place. But the arrests are still going to happen, and the absence of this right is the reason for it."

"But the strike organizers must've known that would happen."

"We have to think long term," says Dalhon, "and be satisfied with a part of our demands being met at this time."

"I don't want to hear it."

"We must prepare for what comes after, which means organizing at the level of individual factories—"

"I said, I don't want to hear it!"

Her shout is so loud Juryong herself glances around, afraid someone is watching. It is, however, the middle of the day, and most of the houses are empty.

"You better run," says Juryong, "before I stuff those shoes of yours in your mouth."

Dalhon looks back at Juryong's deathly glare before standing up straight.

"It's that courage of yours we value," he says, "you'll see."

★

See what? That he was right? Or whether I'll really join his organization? Whatever he meant, she doesn't want to think about it. Just the thought of his pale face and his arrogant Kyongong accent makes her want to scream.

But Dalhon ends up being at least partially right. The police raid the strike headquarters, beating up and arresting the union officers, who do not put up any resistance. Juryong hears of this the day after it happens. At least Kang Deoksam managed to flee and is preparing to negotiate with the Chamber of Commerce. Bourgeois as they are, it is said that at least the Chamber of Commerce are learned people and eager about negotiating their terms.

Each factory sends a representative into the negotiation team. Perhaps out of a principle of fairness, Kang Deoksam and the strike organization officers are excluded from this group. Of the people who are not officers, they try to send someone who can read and who has some position in their factory, who turn out to be mostly men. The Pyongyang Chamber of Commerce team and the strikers team come up with a compromise of the demands. Of the refusal to lower wages, the rate of reduction is lowered from 17 to 10 percent, and ten demands are fully accepted while the rest are either rejected or partially accepted. Not a grand victory, but not a defeat, either. The strikers are divided on whether to accept the compromise.

Juryong leans toward rejection. It's her opinion that the strikers-side negotiators agreed to the compromised demands so quickly because they had no idea how bad the factory women had it. She keeps thinking of Jeong Dalhon insisting they needed to accept a compromise. Nonsense! Not when they had fought so hard.

Just a day after the negotiations, the police issue them with an order: accept the police's terms for ending the strike and not the Chamber of Commerce's.

Another emergency rally is held. The festive atmosphere of the first one is completely replaced with aggressive and accusatory slogans. Criticism is poured on the senseless intervention of the police and their even more senseless terms, not to mention the factory owners who have unconditionally accepted the terms, and there are even declarations of no-confidence on the incompetent strikers-side negotiators who had accepted the Chamber of Commerce's terms with nary a fight.

Juryong knows that underneath the dark, bubbling tar of gloom, anger simmers. She can't help but knowing, as she herself is furious.

Since the emergency rally, there is a rally every day. Factories with strong union membership declare sit-in protests and barricade their places of work, but police raids make them impossible to sustain.

Throughout all this, Juryong rubs her dry face with her rough hands and keeps mumbling, "What an awful mess this all is."

★

In the beginning of September, the strikers declare an end to the strike. They try to hold one last rally to commemorate the end, but the police break it up. The police from the outside and the intractable conflict between strikers, officers, and negotiators on the inside bring the strike to an end after a month.

The Pyongyang Rubber Business Association, which represents the factory owners, unconditionally accepts the police's terms that are far inferior to the initial list of demands or even the negotiated version. After 2,300 rubber workers participating for a month with around sixty arrests and almost a tenth of all participants fired, what they've gained for it is not enough. Pitiful, in fact.

Having returned to the factory after a month away, Juryong fiddles around at her workstation as if she's forgotten how to do her job. When she looks up, all she sees are the bereft faces of her fellow workers.

Even the foreman listlessly wanders between the lines of workstations. Juryong had seen his face in the parade and around the strikers' tent. She was never taught how to act when someone she couldn't bear call comrade appears on her side. A part of her had wanted to run up to him and slap him on the back of the head saying, "How dare you show your face in a place like this," but another part of her had to concede he was also a laborer in the end, a thought that confused her. To see that man experiencing the same despair at how badly the strike had ended makes her think she's in a strange dream. But the negotiators chosen from the factories had been men like him. From Juryong's factory, it had been a man who worked in both the assembly and roller divisions. She has never met this man, but she finds herself hating him more than she hates the foreman.

On her way home from another day of working in a fog, she bumps into the only man in the world who could possibly make her even more miserable in this moment.

"Hello," he says.

"Leave and go about your business."

"But you are my business, Juryong-ssi. I am here to see you."

Juryong ignores him and continues walking her way. Behind her, Dalhon follows like a puppy.

Furious, Juryong turns around and barks, "What is the matter with you men!"

"What do you mean?"

"Nine-tenths of the workers in the factory are women, why did you send in a man to negotiate and ruin our strike? What a laugh they must've had with the Chamber of Commerce, what friends they must've found in them! I'm sure it's because those men were treated better than any of us women were treated. They had no idea how desperate we were in our struggle!"

"I know you are angry, but let's get one thing straight. This strike failed because of the police, not because of the negotiators. They're not experienced and were probably overwhelmed, but they, too, are part of the struggle. It's strange, all the internal conflict with this strike. More resentment toward the negotiators than the police, which also seems to be the case with you."

The sight of his calm face laying down this dispassionate assessment frustrates Juryong so much she pounds her chest.

"How wonderful for you," she says, "that you are so clever. Everything turned out the way you said it would. Does that make you happy?"

"Do I look happy? All I did was prepare myself for what I foresaw would happen. Because we always have to ready ourselves for the next fight. Look here, I'm ready to give the rest of my life to this cause. Whether Juryong-ssi believes it or not, the failure of this strike cuts me to the bone."

The mention of the next fight catches Juryong's interest.

He's right. There is always a next fight. And surely the world hadn't ended just because the strike had. They just had to fight again. To fight until they won. Except everyone is so exhausted they didn't have the energy to talk about what comes next. Yet. Right now. But they will talk about it—soon.

"The next fight?"

Juryong tries to say this as nonchalantly as possible, but she cannot hide the tremble in her voice.

"That's what I said. Didn't I mention it before? We need to change the narrative so that each factory strengthens their union organizing."

"So what is it, exactly that you want from me?"

Relieved she finally speaks his language, Dalhon grins.

"We want you to join the preparatory committee of the Pyongyang Red Labor Union."

5

She seems to be born to fight.

Dalhon wrote this in his diary the day he first met Juryong.

The more he got to know her, the stronger he felt this. On the first day of their general strike, on the third time he sought her out, he felt it more than ever.

"Pyongyang Red... what?"

"The preparatory committee for the Pyongyang Red Labor Union."

"What kind of a name is that? When they say a long name means a short life for babies." Juryong is so shocked by what tumbles out of her own mouth that she clams up. It's just too ingrained in her a habit to snap back at Dalhon.

Dalhon's shoulders shake as he laughs. "Any preparatory committee is hopefully short-lived. Because the real goal is to establish a real workers' union."

"And what kind of organization is that, exactly?"

"Our goal is to enlighten laborers through the labor union movement to hasten the socialist revolution."

Juryong's eyes narrow. "Is that... like the liberation movement?"

"A very open question. You can say they're similar, but our objective is not the liberation of Korea. Of course, as a socialist,

I hope for Korea's liberation and yearn for the banishment of the Japanese imperialists as part of the liberation of our workers, but a socialist revolution is—"

"You've lost me."

"It's not a liberation movement for the nation; it's one for laborers."

"So it *is* about liberation."

"… I suppose so."

Juryong thinks for a moment.

"Well," she says in a softer tone, "I don't think Dalhon-ssi is such a bad person after all. The Pyongyang Red… Fine, let me think about it."

"Thank you. I'll come again tomorrow. Until you agree to join, I'll come see you every day."

Juryong waves her hand, walks away, then suddenly turns back.

"But why do you keep coming to see a mean and nasty woman like me? An intellectual like you and a rubber factory worker like me, the others will laugh if you say we joined the same cause."

"Do you care so much about what others say about you? In *The Romance of the Three Kingdoms*, Liu Bei is said to have gone to Zhuge Liang's house three times to beg him to join."

"Don't use such fancy examples at me. I have no education and can't understand you."

Dalhon smiles and shrugs. Juryong wonders what that's supposed to mean as she turns around and heads home.

As promised, Dalhon shows up at the end of her workday. Yesterday she was too full of rage to care about what others would say, but today she's afraid of people like Hong who might spread unsavory rumors about her and some male intellectual. She lets him trail behind her until they get to a street with few pedestrians.

"I said all right, you can stop following me now."

"All right? Do you mean you'll join our organization? May I take it as a yes?"

He already smiles a lot, but now his eyes are positively radiant. Was she really worth that much to him? The thought embarrasses her so much she wants to retract her assent.

"Yes. I thought about it a lot when I went home. We need help if we're going to put together a proper labor union. And also, I want to apologize for how I behaved to you."

"Not at all, not at all. I am grateful, so grateful."

It looks like he might hug her. But why would he care so much about a silly little factory girl that he would endure such insults from her and be so thankful now? What if he finds out how unworthy she is of his high esteem? How disappointed he would be. Even though she's thought a lot about her decision, she still feels much dread about it.

However Juryong feels, Dalhon is overjoyed. He acts like Juryong's decision is akin to the launch of the Red Labor Union itself, and he's keen to immediately take her to the temporary headquarters of the Korean Communist Party.

Juryong hasn't been in many Western-style buildings. The factory, train stations, the coffee house, the cinema… Well, the Chinese jail was also Western, wasn't it? And what is a party, and what is a party headquarters? The building makes her think of how Juryong and Dalhon live in the same city of Pyongyang but move through different worlds.

For the first time in her life, she sits in what is called a seminar. They read a book by a Russian woman named Kollontai and do something called a debate over it. Dalhon mostly listens, but Juryong notices that every time he pipes up to say a few words, the others turn to him with immediate deference and even reverence. Their admiration for him is palpable and hard to overlook.

"Is this Jeong Dalhon such a great man?" she asks the person sitting next to her, who blanches at the question.

"I suppose you don't know yet. Comrade Jeong Dalhon is a star among the youth of the Korean Workers' Party. An elite, sent to the Communist University in Moscow by recommendation from the Party. He returned last year and was in Hamheung until recently."

An intellectual among intellects. Suddenly intimidated, Juryong drops her gaze onto the handout she had been given at the beginning of the seminar. Dalhon either senses her discomfort or just wants to tease her because he says, "And now we should listen to what our sole female comrade, Kang Juryong-ssi thinks of all this."

"What? Well, I, it's not as if I've read this book…" Juryong tries to wave away the attendees' attention but Dalhon persists.

"You looked so intently at the handout! It doesn't have to be relevant to the seminar, you can just tell us how you feel about attending."

"Well…" Juryong clears her throat. "Well, as Comrade… I mean, Jeong Dalhon-ssi says, I am the only woman here. Which is why I want to ask you all first: Are any of you married?"

Of the seventeen or so men, all but three or four raise their hands.

"Do you feel that your wives have the same ideology as yourselves?"

The men with their raised hands look at each other. It's obvious they are not quite happy with this random woman at their table with her odd questions. Only Dalhon continues to smile and smile.

"Please don't think too much about what I say, I only had this thought looking over the handout, it's my silliness. But I'm not as satisfied with your answers either. It's only my own thought, but I wonder if your wives indeed have the same ideology as you. The sun has set but you are all here and they are keeping house. If I may say so, I don't think any of you have ever paused to think about what ideology your wives might have. You take it for granted that a woman be uneducated and ignorant, and because you're communes or communists or what, you assume your wives would be as well. If I'm wrong, let me know how wrong I am. But even if I'm wrong, you're still here and not your wives, and they don't have this chance to learn like you do. Your wives are at home, waiting to take care of you, just like they've been made to since birth."

The silence is total. Dalhon begins to clap. The young members gathered, reluctantly clap along.

"You're right. And furthermore, here we are reading a book written by a woman on the women's labor movement, but there is only one woman present with us. This is a significant oversight on our part. Especially when the labor movement in Pyongyang is nine-tenths women factory workers, centered around the rubber industry. We need to think more about women and understand them better."

The men who showed distaste when Juryong spoke are now nodding to Dalhon's words. Juryong suppresses her irritation as she joins in the applause for Dalhon.

"So now, my comrades, let us try to become more conscious of our homes and bring our wives to the next seminar."

Dalhon walks Juryong home, as an apology for keeping her with them so late. The silence is so awkward that Juryong speaks whatever is on her mind the whole way.

"This seminar business we had today was very interesting."

"We were lucky today's topic was Kollontai. I hope she inspires you as well. If I may be so bold, I hope Juryong-ssi will become the Kollontai of Korea."

A blush rises on Juryong's cheeks and she turns away. "What a silly notion." A man on the other side of the street points at her and Dalhon.

What's with that stupid bastard?

The pointing man whispers something to the woman next to him and roars with laughter as they walk away. Sure, it's ridiculous that a factory woman and a suited intellectual are walking side by side. Well, by the looks of it, the pointing man is accompanied by a gisaeng, so who's pointing at who? Juryong is so angry she turns around and curses at him.

"You bastard, you're not even fit for dog food!"

Startled, Dalhon covers her mouth which startles Juryong more. Only when she elbows his side does he let go of her.

"What's that about?" she demands as Dalhon rubs his side.

"I'm sorry. But I didn't want to hear you curse like that."

"He's the one who insulted me first, so what does it matter if I curse back?"

"To know how to curse like that means you've lived a life under such abuse. It's my belief that curses have more to do with the dignity of the person speaking them than those receiving them."

Juryong doesn't know what to say. He's right, partly. The curses she just used had once been used on herself. But she doesn't understand why it's wrong to reveal the fact that this had been the life given to her.

"I agree with half of what you say and disagree with the other half."

"There's nothing wrong with that. It's hard enough to fully understand oneself, isn't it?"

Juryong loudly dusts off her sleeves and skirt. "I understand such words even less."

★

She attends a seminar one evening a week and visits the party headquarters building every Sunday. It's rare she ever runs into Dalhon. If she'd known he was such a busy man, would she have been nicer to him? And why had such a busy man bothered to come to her three, four times to make sure she joined them? She wonders this as she sees him come into the building, put a bundle of papers down, pick another bundle up, and walk right out.

She thinks more about what happened on their walk back home that evening than the seminar itself. How the man with the gisaeng on his arm had pointed at her. She had feared being pointed at like that all her life, but wasn't this the first time in her life it ever happened? And it happened because of Dalhon. A woman wearing her old clothes wouldn't warrant a second glance. Juryong might as well be a speck of dust when she's alone, only visible if she happens to sit on freshly laundered sheets. Similar to dust, people frown when they actually notice her. Dalhon made people notice her. This man, as pale and elegant as a crane, had made someone point their finger at blameless her.

But what can be done now, go to Dalhon and demand to know why he walked her home? And doesn't the man who pointed that finger deserve blame as well? He pointed at her while his other arm was around the waist of a gisaeng. Was it right that all this anguish should come from his finger and for her to blame Dalhon for it?

It had happened in a moment. Juryong could've overlooked it. But because she noticed it, that brief moment of humiliation now taunts her day and night.

★

"Busy?"

Dalhon, about to rush out again, throws some attention to Juryong. She ignores him, her eyes fixed on the book in front of her.

"You're reading Kollontai's *Red Love*," he observes as he comes up to her. Juryong closes the book she has been too distracted to really read. "How have you been?"

"The same," she says. "There's no good or bad to it."

"Are you learning much?"

His question reminds her that Dalhon hadn't come to the seminars lately. Where people stare at her for pointing out that strange things were strange and for having questions. Stares that seemed to say, *Of course a woman would say that.*

"What I've learned so far is that the laborer is the greatest and most fundamental class, but the elites just see them as people to educate and lead. That's my latest complaint."

"Wonderful."

A compliment or empty words? He's about to run off.

"I know where Dalhon-ssi is going," Juryong says.

"You do? Where am I going?"

"A factory in Heungnam, to organize and educate. Back and forth between Pyongyang and Heungnam."

Dalhon doesn't say anything for a moment. "You're correct. I've never hid it but never told you, either. I'm passing on the work to my successor and I'll be in Pyongyang permanently soon."

The nitrogen fertilizer factory in Heungnam is the largest factory in all of Korea. Not only was it built on Japanese capital but the Japanese government owns the business outright. Which means the police surveillance there is stronger than in other places. Dalhon and other elites from the Communist University apparently are not as successful there as they had hoped.

"I think you've failed because you're all fancy intellectual elites."

Dalhon scoffs. "We haven't failed yet. You're a little harsh today, aren't you?"

"I might as well say what I have to say. The problem isn't police surveillance or any of that. The problem is that intellectuals like you don't think much of the proletariat. Deep down, you only see us as ignorant masses to educate. But the workers at the factory, they're mostly men, are they not? They probably don't think much of you either, deep down. You have never made something with your own hands and sweat, and yet here you are, ordering them around—"

"All right, I see what you mean." His face, usually all smiles, is hard.

Juryong doesn't stop. "I'm not done. Tell me. You approached me because you needed to hang a sign out front, did you not? The ignorant factory women didn't look like they would listen to the elite men, and you needed a good puppet to put on a show for them?"

"Why are you playing a victim?"

"You're the one who should watch what you say. I'm just being honest."

"Juryong-ssi."

"I can't keep up with you intellectuals, it's too shameful for me."

"Juryong-ssi!"

"How stupid do I look? Looking like this and pretending these great intellects of Pyongyang are my comrades, when you and the others don't even think of me as—"

"That's enough. I said I see what you mean."

Dalhon's voice is cold. She has never heard him sound so cold.

"What do I mean, then?"

"You're right. Completely. I am using you. I approached you from the start to use you. Satisfied?"

Juryong is speechless. She'd been the one to throw her thorny words at him, the thoughts that had bothered her for a long time, but to hear him admit it makes her ears ring.

"We need people like Juryong-ssi. We need you. It *has* to be you. Just as you cannot substitute me, no one can substitute you in the role you play. Is that so wrong? You should use us too. Use me, the organization, as much as you can."

He sighs.

"I've heard you are doing well. That while I was gone, you attended every gathering and participate actively in the discussions. This may sound like flattery, but I couldn't do what you're doing now, even if I wanted to. I can't speak for the factory women or claim to understand what they go through. But you, Juryong-ssi, you can find so many useful things through me. Ideology and theory, these are things that can be picked up."

Juryong's welling tears overflow. Dalhon is disconcerted by her crying. He's used to her rants and discontent, but this is an unexpected side of her. Juryong turns away, and he doesn't know what to do with himself.

"Why the tears? I'm sorry. Please don't cry."

Juryong covers her eyes with her sleeve so she can't see his consternation.

"Don't think little of me for crying. It's only because I can never win with you and that makes me angry. It means nothing else."

"I don't think little of you. And I don't think I've won, either. You are genuinely unique. It's like you were born to fight. Show us what you're made of. Think little of me. Do you understand?"

With her back to him, Juryong manages a nod.

6

By attending every seminar and training session, Juryong gets to
see all sorts of people who work in Pyongyang. As the season
passes, she gets closer to the others on the preparatory committee
for the Red Union. She's worried that others may look down at
her for being uneducated, but it turns out they're textile workers
and security guards and drivers and bricklayers. There are a few
intellectuals and elites like Dalhon, but there are more laborers
like Juryong. Those who studied all the way to high school but
had to quit because they couldn't afford the tuition, those who
are illiterate and have to take in all the education by ear only. Juryong is determined never to judge anyone for the life they'd lived.
Education did not always make someone a better person, and a
lack of it didn't mean someone was bad, either. And she didn't
want to be judged in that way herself.

At the same time, she tries to organize the other workers
at her factory into a future union. Most of them are those who
came out to the general strike, and the rest are those who want to
at least lend moral support, like Ginseng. They promise to save a
small portion of their pay for union tithes. Thanks to the group's
small size, secrecy isn't a big problem.

The company likely will think they're just a bunch of girls
chatting and giggling over foolishness and ignore them when it

was a revolution they were preparing, heatedly and sure. Inside the freezing factory where they had shut off the power, Juryong smiles. If anything, the heat from the rubber forms warms their hands and increases productivity.

Dalhon, who'd been missing since early winter, is to return permanently to Pyongyang in February. The founding of the Red Labor Union is imminent.

"Take this, too," says Juryong as she hands over money she's collected from the factory. Dalhon doesn't ask questions as he snatches it up.

"We'll put it to good use."

"You're not even going to ask what it is?"

"I might say no to it if I knew where it came from, and you'd be angry at me if I said no."

Juryong grins. She's heard that Dalhon, before he became so busy, worked as a load carrier near Daedong Bridge to earn money for the cause. He'd been ashamed, as an intellectual, that he had never done hard labor, and he must be too busy now to earn a bit of extra money to sustain himself.

"We give it to you to support your organizing."

"How could I not know that? Thank you."

Oddly enough, Juryong feels proud of what she's done. Jeong Dalhon is her comrade as well as a teacher, and she's always felt indebted to him. This donation makes her feel as if she's now on equal footing with him. Even as she understood the money would go toward improving the organization she herself was affiliated with.

"But how long are you going to use that silly Kyongong accent of yours? You came to Pyongyang last year, you should know how to speak like this city by now?"

Dalhon smiles uncertainly as he fiddles with the envelope in his hands. Juryong has never seen him like this before.

"I'm from Hamnam," he says, "and my real accent is stronger than yours."

Juryong cackles. "Well let's hear it then, how does a Hamnam person speak?"

"I don't want to. I'm an intellectual, am I not? A real intellectual."

His joke—because it is he who always tells her to not take intellectuals seriously—makes Juryong laugh harder.

★

In April, the founding ceremony for the Red Labor Union is finally held. It's a small affair, attended by about twenty men and women, but their hearts are as hot as the time of the general strike. They read the declaration of solidarity, each speak a few words, and sing "The Internationale" together. The reception afterward lasts until dawn.

"We're going to have to get used to working this late at night," says Dalhon as he escorts Juryong home. "Our organization will be under surveillance of the police. The Empire isn't afraid of guns, they have more of those than we do. What they're afraid of is the spread of ideology. Can there be a scarier thing than the entire working class obtaining a sense of ownership?"

His mention of future activities reminds her of his words when he recruited her, about there being a next fight. "What happens now? Do we strike again? Our comrades in the factory are ready. Shall we make the title of the strike the recovery of our decreased wages?"

Dalhon shakes his head.

"We need a trigger event. Like when the Great Depression two years ago triggered the wage decrease that drew 2,300 rubber workers in Pyongyang to strike. This is history. It's how history is made."

The word "trigger" brings to mind the time when Juryong had her finger on a real trigger. Of when she was so afraid to harm someone by her own hand that her comrade had been wounded. Of when she learned that one needed to pull the trigger when it needed to be pulled.

Her hands turn clammy. She rubs them together as she waits for Dalhon to continue.

"And I dare to think this trigger event is not far off. Our struggle, I have no doubt, will itself be a trigger that will set off someone else's liberation."

★

Dalhon has never been wrong. This time, it's no different. The trigger even came upon them like a thief in the night. So quickly that Juryong wonders if she summoned it with her impatience.

In mid-May, the Pyongyang Rubber Association, a group of rubber factory owners, collectively decided to lower wages once more. Still, in fear of the response of the Rubber Workers Alliance that had instigated the strike years before, they were hesitant to decide when. Once the newspapers printed this, the Pyongwon Rubber Factory immediately announces that their wages are being lowered. A farce. Pyongwon was one of the smaller factories in the city, and the owner wasn't even a member of the Pyongyang Rubber Association. But Juryong instantly understands this is an opportunity, the trigger event.

The day they are informed of their wages being cut, Juryong holds an emergency meeting with the other factory workers, and they begin their protest. The money she had gathered and passed on to Dalhon returns to them in the form of a tent for the protesters. They set up headquarters near the factory, print statements, and post them all over the factory district.

News of the Pyongwon Rubber Factory's strike spreads quickly. In solidarity, workers at factories with owners affiliated with the Pyongyang Rubber Association stage a work stoppage. As the strike goes over three days, the Pyongwon Factory Workers Union change their slogan from "Say no to lower wages!" to "Fair wages or death!" and Juryong's heart swells at this slight yet monumental shift. It should've been their slogan all along.

Late into the night as the strike moves from its fourth day into its fifth, Dalhon visits.

"I am here in solidarity," says his solemn voice.

It was a good thing he spoke, for Juryong could barely recognize him.

"Dalhon-ssi!"

Whether it was to avoid the eyes of the surveillance or because he needed the work, Dalhon has appeared in tattered work clothes, carrying his jige. Juryong, who could barely leave the protest site, was scarcely at her best herself, but Dalhon has always neatly dressed like a gentleman. His current state endears him to her, and she can't help but smile. She realizes she hasn't smiled at all these past few days. There is nothing untoward between her and Dalhon, but she still self-consciously looks about her. Just three or four other workers, sleeping through their shift at the tent.

"How are you, Juryong-ssi? You were so itching to start the fight."

"When did I say I wanted to fight? Who in this world truly wants to fight? Nobody. People don't want to fight, they want to win."

"A very Juryong-ssi thing to say."

Juryong sits him down on a straw mat and sits herself down as well. He drags his jige over to lean against and says, "So, any difficulties so far?"

"What could be difficult? When we're doing this to win."

"Aren't you afraid?"

"I'm afraid someone might die. I'm afraid it might be me, and I'm afraid someone else might die as well. I'm afraid of people who aren't afraid of people dying."

Dalhon doesn't answer.

Juryong tries to lighten her tone. "Still, I'm a woman who's not afraid of anything. Because I've been through it all. I lost my husband early, I lost touch with my family after that, and it wasn't for a long time, but I was in jail once. I've lived through it all already, so what could I possibly be afraid of? I've been through worse than this."

Dalhon listens and says, "Juryong-ssi, people can use themselves up too quickly. You must take care of yourself as well. Take care of yourself now so you can use yourself later."

"Don't worry about me. Dalhon-ssi should worry about himself."

"Everyone in Pyongyang is watching you and the struggle at the Pyongwon factory. This isn't just about you or you forty nine factory workers anymore. I have no doubt you will lead us to the Red Labor Union's first victory."

"Don't you worry about that."

Dalhon gets up and hoists his jige upon his shoulders. Before he slips out of the tent, he turns around and says one more thing to her.

"Don't get hurt."

A slice of night is visible through the half-open tent flap he leaves behind. It's late May, but the winds are still chilly. Juryong feels a sudden sorrow. But the sorrow, if anything, clears her mind. She's barely slept a wink since the beginning of the protest, but she feels more awake than she ever has in her life. She pulls out a large piece of paper, takes out a brush, and begins to write a new statement.

The factory owner responds to their requests for negotiations by calling in the police. The statement she is writing to post on the factory wall becomes useless.

Until this moment, the only time police were called in against protesters was when the factory owner was Japanese. There is something fundamentally different from calling in the police to protect one's property and this situation. The police are not here to protect a small factory owned by a Korean. Their intention is to snuff out any labor movement as is necessary, no matter how small.

The policemen in front of the factory gates number about a hundred. Just forty nine protesters, all women, and half of them with children in their arms, and for that they brought twice as many men.

As always, Juryong slowly walks up to the factory gates. The tent is pitched just a stone's throw away. For the sake of those behind her, she walks with no hesitation and pretends she's unafraid. But she can feel their fear without looking back at them, the way they huddle like frightened rabbits, tentative as they follow her.

Three steps away from the police, she stops and turns around.

"Let's do a sit-in."

As directed, they workers sit in rows of six. Juryong has her back to the police and can only guess at what goes on with them from the faces of the workers as they sit down. She's tried not to look at the police but can't help a glance. At least they don't hold guns, even if they're wielding batons. She steels her back against them once more.

She reads out the statement they couldn't post, in call-and-response fashion with the workers. By the time she's almost done with it, the commanding officer behind her says something in Japanese, and the ground rumbles as the hundred policemen shuffle their feet and get into position. She breaks into a cold sweat but pretends to be unperturbed as she finishes reading out the statement and dismisses the protest. Thankfully, the police do not follow them to the tent.

"Comrades, you sat so excellently in your neat rows. Were you teaching the police a lesson?"

Some of the others in the tent laugh at her joke. Even if the day's protest had only been a couple of hours, their faces are pale with exhaustion. As much as they'd expected the police to intervene, it is quite another thing to see one hundred policemen assembled to intimidate them. Juryong worries about morale.

"We have done nothing wrong," she says loudly to the workers, "and the factory owner here has no clout. Do you understand what that means? The police were deployed to intimidate us, but they have no excuse to arrest us, that's what. And if the factory owner was Japanese, we would've been thrown in jail on the first day of our protest. Comrades, am I right or wrong?"

"Hear, hear!"

They're taken aback by their first sight of police but don't seem to have lost the urge to fight. But now that the police are involved, a clash is inevitable. It's only a matter of when. Juryong hopes no one gets hurt. They can very well win and at the same time sustain heavy losses. The best thing would be to succeed without anyone getting hurt, but that's just like wanting to win without a fight. The worst is if many people are hurt and they fail to stop the wage decrease. As long as they've begun to fight, they have to prevent the worst from happening at all costs.

But things can always get worse, now that the fight has begun.

Juryong hugs herself with her still-shaking arms.

★

The same nonconfrontation happens every day for the next few days. As long as they don't attempt to storm the factory, the police do not intervene with force. Were they being too cautious? Juryong constantly asks herself this. Morale flags. Every day they shout their slogan—"We oppose to the death"—but there's no answer from the factory owner. Is this the point where they have to force an answer, even it means they draw blood?

As Juryong worries over this near the tent, a woman runs toward her. A factory union member? No, someone from the Red Labor Union. She's rushed here to convey some news, but it's hard to tell by her approach if it's good or bad. Juryong's heart beats with dread as she runs to meet her halfway.

"Comrade Kang, something bad has happened," the woman says, out of breath. "Jeong Nagi has been arrested."

Nagi is Dalhon's baby name. They use it as a code name outside the union in case there are spies. Pain grips her body like a giant's hand. Her head and chest aches and her breath is trapped. Maybe it's useful that this feeling is so familiar to her. Juryong controls herself as she chooses the words to say.

"I understand. You should get to somewhere safe, comrade."

"We are fine for now. The ones who've been taken are members of the Korean Communist Party. I thought you should know, as you can't leave your protest."

"Still, be careful."

"I'm more worried about you, Comrade Kang."

Left alone, Juryong stumbles back into the tent, the shock still ringing in her ears and behind her eyes. The union members are sitting inside the small tent, close together. Aside from the ones who have gone home for a moment, there are thirty or so of them in there. The union members go home less and less. Quite a few of them report being followed by suspicious men. They came up with rules for always moving in groups of three, even to return home. The night shift at the tent is now raised to ten. The union members have decided on their own to stay longer.

The sight of their faces turned toward Juryong begin to blur in her vision. She closes her eyes.

"Comrades, I…" She can't form the words as her throat closes. She tries again. "We need to make a decision."

Everyone is quiet as they wait for her to continue. Juryong desperately tries to regain her composure.

"I've been too scared that people would get hurt that I could not suggest what I am about to, but…" She forces herself to say the words. "I intend to stop eating today and begin a hunger strike."

The hunger strike had been a last-resort option for a long time now. Dalhon's arrest broke through her hesitation. They can't keep up this fight for much longer, and she's long resolved to die if need be, rather than surrender.

Her words, once spoken, calm her. The other workers look at each other but say nothing. Juryong takes the moment to put her thoughts in better order before she speaks again.

"As the leader of this protest, I resolve to starve to death rather than accept defeat. Tonight, I shall infiltrate the factory and declare a hunger strike. My comrades, you must spread word of this to every labor organization and workers at the other factories. The police are as tired as we are, there will be a way in."

The woman Hong raises her hand. "I will go with you."

"I as well."

"I'm not going to let hyungnim die of starvation alone, I'm coming."

The hands shoot up like bamboo sprouts.

"At this rate, we should ask those who don't want to hunger strike to raise their hands," someone says, and the tent falls into silent solidarity.

Juryong is moved, but she waves her hands before her in refusal.

"Please don't follow me. We need comrades to survive the hunger strike to fight another day."

"If we're going to die, we might as well die together," someone says, and everyone begins to applaud.

Juryong swallows back her tears to steady her voice.

"Then we shall hunger strike in solidarity and see this struggle to the very end. Comrades, thank you for doing this together."

The applause is loud and long.

★

The workers who had gone home also agree to a hunger strike when they return, and so all forty nine protesters join the effort.

The police only guard the main entrance. At night, merely half of them remain, and even they take turns sleeping. The union members strategize, dividing into teams for the infiltration. Juryong and a few of the smaller members will go through a gap in the walls to open the back gate. They will walk in different groups far away from the factory and enter in staggered intervals. If there are too many people milling about the back gate, it'll arouse suspicion.

Juryong and two others in her group easily slip through a gap in the wall. Briefly, Juryong thinks of the hole she once discovered in their rabbit hutch in Gando. They had counted and counted the rabbits, thinking it odd that they kept disappearing, and it turned out they'd dug a hole under the wooden fencing. Juryong could just about slip her hand through it. She thought it was how the rabbits got out, but her parents thought it was a weasel, which explained why a hole would appear so quickly. But if it had been a weasel, there would've been blood. And domesticated rabbits are so sensitive that some die of fright simply from the sight of a weasel entering the hutch. Juryong still thinks she's right. No matter how weak and vulnerable a beast, they will still find a way to survive.

Opening the back gate isn't difficult. It takes about an hour for all of them to infiltrate. The members who have successfully entered the factory move slowly against the wall as to not attract the attention of the police outside. Juryong lays a hand on her beating heart as she glances out the front gate. The police are a few steps beyond it, but her fear and the darkness make it seem like they are right in front of her. Juryong gestures toward a comrade who stands in the shadows across from her.

The factory gate is wide enough for two trucks to go through side by side. There's a smaller gate for people right next to it. At her signal, the comrade by the side gate quietly closes it. The clang it makes as it locks makes their hearts drop. Silence follows. They are not caught, it seems. The workers, moving from shadow to shadow, enter the factory.

Even now, when the machines aren't running, the air reeks of processed rubber, toxic chemicals, and the lubricants used on the rollers. The darkness seems to intensify the stench. It's not a good idea to turn on the lights, so Juryong determines who's inside by touching each of their hands and hearing them speak their name. Once she's sure of all forty eight names, she says her own.

"We have all successfully entered the factory," she says to them once they've gathered around her. Their dark forms look like multiple shadows extending from the feet of one person.

"Our hunger strike begins now."

7

The police are not aware until the strikers gather in the front yard of the factory when the sun rises. It's almost silly they bothered to work so quietly.

Juryong turns toward the gate and shouts, "Hear this, Pyongwon factory owner and police!"

"Hear this, Pyongwon factory owner and police!" the strikers repeat.

The police realize the strikers have left the tent and are inside the factory. Their commanding officer says something in Japanese and they all turn around to face the factory. Juryong tamps down on her fear and shouts, "From this day on, we the Rubber Workers Union of Pyongwon Rubber Factory—"

She pauses so the other strikers can repeat her. The strikers see the police as well, but their voices betray no fear. Perhaps their fear is drowned out by the loudness of their determination.

"If the factory owner does not heed our demands in negotiation—"

The commanding officer orders the police to advance. As bravely as the workers stand in the middle of the yard, the march of the police strikes fear into their hearts.

"We resolve to hunger strike!"

"We resolve to hunger strike!"

Juryong takes a breath before the next line.

"The factory owner must cancel the wage decrease and negotiate!"

The union workers repeating this sound more uncertain than before.

Juryong sends them into the factory before rushing in herself and locks the door. The workers push the machines against the door as a barricade. They scatter and push other bulky equipment against the barricade to reinforce it and sit or lean against it.

Night falls without incident.

The workers doze, exhausted both from lack of sleep the previous night and also their hunger strike. Juryong's body doesn't listen to her except to sit on the floor and lean against a wall. The hunger strike can't last long, she thinks.

From the outside, a shout. Possibly a call, an order. It comes from nearby.

It's finally about to happen.

Petrified, the union members grip each other's hands. Some wake those who are too tired and hungry to have heard the police.

Juryong shouts, "Let's sing! 'The Eldest Daughter at the Rubber Factory.'"

"The early morning commuter train—"

Before they could finish the first verse, they hear something large and blunt smash against the main entrance doors. It thuds against their backs as they lean against the barricade. The people cry as they hug each other. There's an odd number of them, so there's no one to hold Juryong.

A window smashes in the dark. Juryong dimly sees a police baton neatly knocking and scraping off glass shards from each side of the window. A lamp flashes in and out of the window.

Juryong shouts, "Comrades, let us link arms and lie on the floor!"

As frightened as they are, they move as if under a trance. A black boot appears on the broken-in window frame. The police beat the people who have lain down and linked arms, dismantle the barricade, and open the door. Juryong, who stands in the middle of it all, shouts at the police.

"Don't beat us with your batons when we don't resist! We've done nothing wrong!"

Three policemen rush at her and grab her arms and legs. As she twists and turns, they carry her outside and throw her out onto the yard.

The factory is in chaos. Linked arms are forced apart, workers are pulled out by their hair, others by their armpits, and still others carried overhead and thrown outside like sacks of grain. Juryong tries to crawl away and run back, but she's caught. The police don't care if they tear her clothes and expose her skin, they continue to carry people out of the factory like they're finished rubber shoes. One hundred police to suppress forty-nine women. Juryong is beside herself from the injustice.

"You bastards!" she shouts. "I wouldn't be satisfied if I chewed you up between my teeth!" Her face is a mess of dirt and tears, and what she feels between her teeth is sand.

The women thrown out of the factory immediately get up and run back inside. Even as they're thrown out again, they rush right back. Juryong gets up, wipes her dirty face, and shouts, "Comrades! You must go back to the protest tent! You have to save yourselves for another—"

The women cry as they keep running back into the factory, not heeding Juryong's words. Juryong goes from one person lying on the ground by the gate to another, whispering to them they must flee. At least the police seem more intent in retaking the factory than making arrests. But who knows when they'll change course.

Outside the gates, the police are knocking down their tent. It's like watching the collapse of her hopes.

"You worthless son of a pig, let go of Deoggie!" The woman Hong hangs from the neck of one of the police and holds onto a young woman named Deoggie. The two women are both thrown outside the gate.

Juryong rushes to the woman Hong and helps her back up. She tells her to go back home. The woman Hong stares at the factory, then at Juryong, then at the collapsed protest tent, and her face breaks into tears. Instead of going home, she goes to the protesters thrown outside the gates, helps them up, and tells them to go home, just like Juryong is doing.

After about an hour of fighting, everyone has been pushed out of the factory. The police secure the grounds and come out of the front gates. The workers who linger at the gates step back to avoid the police and eventually disperse.

It's the end.

Juryong also turns her back to the factory and swallows her sour-and-salty spit seeping through her gritted teeth. Her throat is swollen, and she can't swallow properly.

8

Juryong wanders the streets of Pyongyang at night. She had moved out of her rented room when she set up the strikers' tent. With Dalhon and the other comrades of the Red Union arrested, she can't go to the temporary offices of the party, either. She saw the tent being dismantled right in front of her. And the union workers had all clung to the struggle against the wishes of their families, so she can't ask them for shelter, either.

Run away. You have to run away.

She wonders if this truly is the best time to return to Gando after all. A useless thought. It's simply a wish to have somewhere to go to. A desire for such a place to be as far away and difficult a journey as possible.

A desire that's clouding her mind.

But if not that, then what am I to do with my life?

I'm hungry.

Juryong scoffs at herself. You began your hunger strike only yesterday, and you're already complaining about hunger?

But she really is hungry. And what did it matter if she went on hunger strike when no one cares that she did? She is so hungry that she could eat the sand on the Daedong's riverbank and die from it happy.

Die from it happy.

All right.

Let's die.

I'll just die.

The thought brings her peace. That's it, that's all I need to do, die. The harsh thoughts in her mind settle down and her torn heart feels as if it's fusing back together. She hadn't felt this calm when she decided to starve herself. What does that mean?

And how shall I die?

The dark paved road is sporadically lit by arched streetlamps. Juryong uses all of her might to keep her tears in as she walks. The only thing she has decided at this point is to die, but every face she has ever known comes rushing into her thoughts. She shakes her head at them.

Leave me alone. Please leave me alone. You never helped me when I tried to live, don't stop me from trying to die.

She wakes up the draper with her knocking at his door.

"It's an emergency. I need a length of cloth."

The draper rubs his eyes and chooses for her a roll of Japanese cotton, not forgetting to mention how strong and high quality it is. Juryong gives him all her money. Tugging at the cloth and making sure it won't tear, Juryong leaves the draper's shop. It wouldn't do if it failed to kill her.

Where shall I die?

The Daedong River is before her. She can't hang herself at a river. Well, there was the Daedong Bridge, but there's enough foot traffic even at this hour and the pedestrians would stop her. If not the river, then the mountain. Juryong turns to stare up at Geumsusan Mountain. She walks. Despite the lateness of the night, there are people about. Even two men with gisaeng women on their arm. She scoffs, but thinks she should try emptier streets.

She sees a copse of trees and goes toward them. Thinking of her body hanging from the branches of these cherry blossom trees in full bloom makes her tear up and smile at the same time. Let it be known that I wanted to die somewhere beautiful as part of my last bit of vanity. But the washed diapers drying on its branches don't really make a pretty a place to die. It's when Juryong is tying the end of her cloth into a knot when she has a thought.

If I'm going to die, I should let people know it's because of the bad deeds of the factory owners of Pyongwon Rubber.

She could leave a suicide note but she has no pen or paper. She's also spent all her money on the cloth.

Ah, well.

Juryong tests the rope she has fashioned and slips her head into the noose. It's so long that even when she's kneeling there's too much slack. It's so absurd she laughs until her belly aches.

What a weak little thing I am. Look at how much I fear death.

She sighs and takes off the noose. As she adjusts the length of the rope, she changes her mind.

What would people think if I kill myself here without leaving a suicide note? Would people even care to know my name? Why would they, if all I am is another foolish woman who wanted to die?

After some thinking, she winds up her cloth and wedges it under her arm.

Let's die in the most beautiful spot in Pyongyang. There, I will shout at the people in my own words, give them my reason for dying, and then kill myself for the whole world to see.

The refrain of "The Internationale" rings in her head.

In the dead of night, Juryong climbs up to Eulmilbong Peak and stands on the terrace of Eulmildae Pagoda. She remembers how she and Okkie never got to the top when they came together.

It takes a bit more thinking to get up onto the roof of the Eulmildae. Juryong twists the fabric this way and that. She finds a rock and ties it to the end of the fabric. She throws it. It takes several tries for the rock to land on the roof. She tests the rope with her weight. The silliness of her own actions makes her laugh.

Even if I died slipping off that roof, I'd still have accomplished what I desired—why do I fear death?

Juryong uses the twisted fabric to scale the wall of the Eulmildae. In case someone tries to follow her, she winds the cotton around her arm after she makes it up to the roof.

Light begins to dawn. It's a long way down. The thought of rolling off the roof and maiming herself is not enough to prevent her from dozing off. She hadn't had a decent night's sleep since joining the strikers, not to mention how she hadn't had a moment of rest since beginning her hunger strike. The wind makes her shiver. Juryong wraps the cotton around herself.

★

"Look, there's a woman up there!"

Juryong is jolted awake by the cries of people staring up at her. She can see others trekking up the mountain path to Eulmilbong, like ants in the distance. Morning hikers.

The sun is already far above the horizon and her forehead is beaded with sweat. Juryong takes off the cotton fabric and stands up, prompting a collective cry of concern from the people below. "I'm calling the firemen! I'm calling the police!" some shout as they run down the mountain path.

"My dear fellow citizens! I am Kang Juryong, and I work at the Pyongwon Rubber Factory!"

The voice that issues from Juryong's throat is as loud and clear as ever. Her own words have the power to make her limbs cease from trembling. Swept up in her own oratory, Juryong pleads her case. She feels she is not her own person. She feels something that is larger, more just, and greater than herself speaking through her.

"Look towards Seonkyori past the Daedong Bridge! That's where my workplace is, the Pyongwon Rubber Factory. When the factory informed us they were cutting our wages, forty nine workers formed a union to fight against their decision!"

So many gawkers have gathered that all she sees below is a crowd.

"We are ready to give up our lives for the struggle! And I, too, shall leave this roof only in death."

The refrain of "The Internationale" plays in her mind.

'Tis the final struggle...

"My fellow citizens, please listen to what I am risking my life to tell you! I plead with you, on behalf of my comrades, the forty nine strikers, the 2,300 rubber workers, and all the working women of Korea, to listen to what I say..."

REVERSAL

"Number 121. You have a visitor."

Dalhon can't believe his ears. It's been several seasons since his sham trial and this is the first time someone has visited him in prison. He'd given up on it by then. Several of the Red Labor Union members had been arrested with him so there's really no one to visit him, and Dalhon being in a leadership position, it was likely any visitation requests would be denied as well.

Dalhon rubs his eyes when he steps into the visitation room. "Juryong-ssi?"

A mistake. The woman wears her hair in an old-fashioned bun. She's about the same age and is dressed shabbily. She's someone he doesn't know. The woman hesitantly gets up and introduces herself before she sits down again.

"I'm Samnyuh, Juryong's friend. We went to the same factory together. Ryongie used to call me Ginseng."

So that's why the visit was granted. A woman who seems above all ideological suspicion.

"Please excuse me. It's been such a long time since I've seen anyone who is not in a prisoner's or guard uniform. So, how did it go? I hear so little news from the outside."

"We won."

Dalhon claps his hands like a child. "What did I tell you! I knew she was a winner!"

Ginseng glances at the guard and takes out a small bundle of papers from her sleeve.

"These are some articles about Ryongie I've collected. She's... been in a lot of papers. Look, I'm not good at speaking... Please take them, quickly."

The guard must've seen her pass it on, but she likely bribed him beforehand. Dalhon slips the bundle deep into his sleeve and turns a calm face to her.

"I've heard a lot about you, Jeong Dalhon-ssi." Ginseng looks like she's about to say more, but instead she stands up.

"Where are you going? There's still some time left. Please talk to me a bit. You've no idea how long it's been that I've seen a civilian—"

Despite his entreaty, Ginseng walks out of the visiting room. Strange.

Dalhon has an uneasy feeling as he fondles the bundle of paper in his sleeve. If it's news of victory, Juryong could've come herself.

Is she in jail as well? It's a possibility.

Dalhon feels a bitterness in his mouth as he gets up to leave the visitation room.

★

Facing a corner, Dalhon takes out the papers Ginseng gave him and unfolds them. The first article is an interview by a reporter named Muho Jungin. "Factory Woman on the Eulmildae: Interview with the Woman Warrior." What a title! His mouth gapes wider and wider as he reads on. He ends up in laughter.

Kang Juryong, the first labor activist in Korea to stage a high-altitude protest. I knew I picked a winner.

His pride in her warms his heart.

The other articles tell the same story. Chronicles in the factory woman Kang's fight. How she protested on the roof of the Eulmildae for hours. How the Japanese police set up a net below and pushed her off the roof into it. How she continued her hunger strike in jail for four days, shouting slogans against the lowering of the workers' wages.

I told you so, I told you that you were born to fight. That you are special.

He can't help smiling. His heart swells, his eyes tear.

As soon as she was released, she returned to the factory and lay herself down in front of the bus ferrying new rubber workers, immediately returning to a protest. She managed to pull the factory owner into a negotiation and made him cancel the wage decrease, but could not negotiate for the fired workers to return to work, and ended up without getting her own job back.

The articles that follow make Dalhon's heart alternate from white-hot to ice-cold, like a bit of steel being forged. But the human heart, unlike steel, does not become harder from forging.

After this half-victory, Juryong is found out as a member of the Red Labor Union and thrown in jail. For a year, she undergoes repeated hunger strikes until she is released due to sickness.

The last article deals with Juryong's death.

Dalhon gets to his feet. He pounds the wall again and again, wailing. The other prisoners try to calm him, but he struggles against them, inconsolable. They come to fisticuffs and Dalhon is thrown into solitary confinement.

★

It's not the decreasing of wages for the forty nine of us that we think is important. What is truly important is that this decrease will lead to decreases for all 2,300 rubber workers in Pyongyang. That's why we will fight to the death against it.

If my one body should die for the 2,300 of my comrades to survive, how could it not be worthwhile? The greatest bit of learning I have ever received is that there is no higher honor than to sacrifice one's life for the greater good. That's why I climbed this roof, with the readiness to die. Until the Pyongwon Rubber Factory owner comes before me and cancels his plan to decrease wages, I shall never walk off this roof on my own two feet. If our wage decrease isn't canceled, then I shall consider it an honor to die for the laboring class who struggle underneath the boot of the capitalists.

So everyone, please do not think to force me from this roof. If anyone so much as places a ladder against the roof, I shall jump off and end my life.

★

In solitary, Dalhon rereads Juryong's speech again and again. He can't put a finger on why he feels so much anguish. The sadness of having lost a comrade? The guilt that if it weren't for the Red Labor Union, Juryong would still be alive? That throughout her struggle, he hadn't helped her for any of it? The regret, so much regret.

Dalhon rereads the articles in reverse chronological order. He does this again and again. He reads until it begins to feel like he experienced it all himself.

Dead Juryong, after suffering for two months, goes to the hospital. In this first and last hospital visit of her life, she's diagnosed with dyspepsia and neurasthenia. She walks backwards from the hospital and into jail. A year, and she's negotiating with the factory owner, laying herself down in front of the bus to demand the reinstatement of the fired strikers, goes into jail where she holds hunger strikes, and walks out of there backwards. She jumps up from the net and lands on the Eulmildae's roof.

The sun sets in the east and Juryong climbs down from the roof. Dalhon closes his eyes as hot tears pour down.

That's where it all begins.

The moonlight makes the white cloth glow. She grabs that light and climbs up to the roof like a seonnyuh fairy in a children's tale. Dalhon, hesitant in ruining that beautiful scene, finally calls out, "Don't go up there! You'll die if you go up there!"

Juryong answers him. That she knows.

Dalhon stares at her helplessly, this woman refuses to listen to him even in his imaginings. She holds on to that cloth like it's a beam of light bringing her up into heaven. Even when her face betrays her fear. Even as she wants to live, burning with a desire, stronger than anyone else in the world, to live.

Someone shouts toward her sleeping form on the roof.

There's a woman up there.

AUTHOR'S NOTE

I said *fight*, even though I could not say what it was we were fighting. I felt that she challenged those around her while loving them at the same time. As no one had called my name for a long time either, I knew what that felt like. I wanted to reach out to her, this woman who had died before I could meet her.

I will not lose my way again. Nor will I die. To those I dared to be kind to, I give a promise that outpaces me into the future.

In this book, my name shall always stand beside hers.

ISBN (paperback): 978-1-917126-21-2
ISBN (ebook): 978-1-917126-22-9
A catalogue record for this book is available from the British Library.
Acquiring Editor: Kristen Vida Alfaro
Art Direction: Kristen Vida Alfaro
Copy Editor: Alyea Canada
Cover Art and Design: Amandine Forest
Line Editor: Jein Han
Managing Editor: Mayada Ibrahim
Marketing Manager: Trà My Hickin
Proofreader: Merray Gerges
Publisher and Director: Kristen Vida Alfaro
Publishing Assistant: Phương Anh
Rights Director: Julia Sanches
Made with Hederis
Printed and bound by Clays Ltd, Elcograf S.p.A.

한국문학번역원

This book is published with the support of the Literature Translation Institute
of Korea (LTI Korea)

ABOUT TILTED AXIS PRESS

Tilted Axis Press is an independent publisher of contemporary literature by the Global Majority, translated into or written in a variety of Englishes.

Founded in 2015, our practice is an ongoing exploration into alternatives to the hierarchisation of certain languages and forms of translation, and the monoculture of globalisation.

We focus on contemporary translated fiction and also publish poetry and non-fiction. Our editorial vision, Translating Waters, is shaped by the complex movement of language, stories, and imaginations. Often fugitive and always trailblazing, our authors and translators challenge how we read, what we think, and how we view the world.

Building and nourishing community is part of our publishing practice. Inspired by the Afro-Asia Writers' Association, literary collectives, and grassroots organisations, we seek collaborative and interdisciplinary projects that expand what constitutes the literary and build on existing solidarities across the globe.

tiltedaxispress.com
@TiltedAxisPress